CRACKS *in the* MIRROR

Sometimes forgiveness is not an option

JAMES J. SMITH

 SEASON Press LLC

Kalamazoo, Michigan

Published in collaboration with
Fortitude Graphic Design and Printing, and Season Press LLC.
Cover and book designed by Sean Hollins
Consultant Editor Sonya Bernard-Hollins

Cracks in the Mirror/James J. Smith

p. cm.
ISBN-13: 978-1-7328-3993-9

1. Short Stories— Relationships 2. Family 3. Social Science

First Edition

10 9 8 7 6 5 4 3 2 1

Printed in the United States of America

DEDICATION

To all aspiring writers whose works have yet to be brought to life by putting pen to paper. Share with the world the thoughts in your mind and the desires of your heart. Make the world a better place for having been inspired by your words of truth, hope, and understanding. Shine your light by way of bringing blank pages to reality so the rest of us need not stumble in darkness.

JJS

CRACKS *in the*
MIRROR

Sometimes forgiveness is not an option

JAMES J. SMITH

INTRODUCTION

The journey of life takes all of us to many places and exposes us to many things along the way in our travels. In addition to the places we encounter on this road we call life, are people we form bonds with or relationships. Some of these relationships are by choice, like a best friend, husband, or wife. Some are not of our own choosing, like a brother, sister, or other family members. Some are ones we have literally made, like a son or daughter, or ones we didn't get to decide in, like who we would be born too.

Regardless, mother, father, sister, brother, husband, wife, or son and daughter, best friend, etc., all have one thing in common. They all are human. And because of that shared trait, they are all imperfect and make mistakes. Because they make mistakes as a result of being human, they will, from time to time, disappoint those who are closest to them. Not because they want to intentionally hurt the ones that love them and that they love, but because of human weaknesses and imperfections.

For different people, it's different things. It's greed for someone whose love of money is stronger than their love for a brother. It's a young father who didn't have the maturity and the strength to be the father he needed to be to his children. Whatever the thing is that broke the relationship when it's put back together—more times than not, it's never the same.

Are there exceptions to the rule? Sure. But very few. "After you Put Back the Pieces (I'll Still Have a Broken Heart)." Those words from the song of the same title by Motown legends, Smokey Robinson and the Miracles, says it all. Those broken pieces of the relationship—the ones we try to make fit in its original place—are the ones most difficult to repair. It's difficult because after we put the relationship back together outwardly, the pain often remains inside...and those are the cracks in the mirror we always feel and see.

CHAPTER 1
Richard & Betty

Richard and Betty were childhood sweethearts. They grew up together on the same street and went to the same schools. If ever there were "two peas in a pod," they were it. All they ever heard from neighbors and friends while they were growing up was how the two of them were meant to be together. More importantly, even as children, Richard and Betty believed it too.

They only had eyes for each other and everyone knew that. Richard was very good in sports, especially basketball. As he got older and bigger, his skills improved as well. By his junior year in high school, college scouts were checking him out. The future as he saw it was right in front of him: graduate from high school, marry the love of his life, get a basketball scholarship to a top college (and the ultimate ending), the NBA! Yeah, he had it all figured out and nothing could stop this dream from becoming a reality. It was his destiny, as he saw it.

Betty on the other hand, was quite close to her family, particularly her mother who had a history of heart disease. Even as a child Betty remembered the pain-filled days and nights her mother would suffer through. Loving Richard gave her an outlet. He was her oasis in a desert of despair and fear, as far as her mother's condition was concerned.

She loved Richard with every fiber of her being, but what she feared most was moving away from her mother. When Richard decided on a college she would have to make a decision too. He would want her to go with him and she didn't know if she could leave her mother just like that. For the moment, she put it out of her mind.

As predicted, college offers came pouring in and Richard was overwhelmed by the whole situation. Betty tried to get a fix on where Richard's head was in terms of what colleges he was considering.

"Have you narrowed it down to any?"

Looking up from the pile of offers, Richard said, "I'm thinking about UCLA or maybe the University of Miami in Florida, somewhere warm. You'd like that, wouldn't you?"

With a half-smile, Betty replied, "Sure baby, whatever you decide."

"It's not just about what I decide Betty, it's also about what you want too."

"O.K. Richard," Betty said as she got up from the dining room table and left the room. *Both of those choices are too far away from Philadelphia and my mother*, she thought.   True to the script that Richard had written in his mind, soon after high school graduation they were married. Richard honored his bride's wish and moved into her mother's house. Betty could see the handwriting on the wall, the time was fast approaching for Richard to make a decision. After he decided on a school—neither one of which she was happy about—what was she going to do?

***

As Betty stood at the sink washing dishes, Richard admired her in the jeans that hugged her figure like they were painted on her. He walked up behind her and placed his arms around her.

"Baby, I've made my choices, UCLA and Miami. I'm going down to Florida for a visit, and later to UCLA. What do you think?"

Betty couldn't say what she really thought. She knew how important this was to him. His life-long dream was becoming reality. How could she stand in the way of that?

"That's great honey," she said, her back still to him to conceal her tears. "When are you leaving for Miami?"

"I got my plane ticket so I'll be leaving in the morning."

"Are you all packed?" she asked as she placed dishes in the drying rack.

"Just about. I got some odds and ends to get, but the major things are done."   After letting the dish water out of the sink, Betty turned around and kissed Richard. "Well, I guess that's that, isn't it?"

"What do you mean by that?" Richard asked with a puzzled look on his face.   "Nothing." Before he could say another word, Betty went upstairs to see about her mother, and drown her sorrow in more of her tears.

***

Richard took a cab to the airport. He could see Betty was upset about him going, eventhough she didn't say so. He had been with her all of his life, so he knew what she was feeling even if it wasn't communicated in words. When he arrived in Miami it was 70 degrees, not bad for a February day, and a far cry from the 27 degrees he left in Philly. Representatives from the university met him and showed him the campus. It was a beautiful campus, but most of all it was warmer than back home.

Miami wanted him and he knew it, so he pushed the envelope as far as he could push it. Whatever he asked for they agreed to, even things he didn't really want. The coaches were cool and the team was good, but he wasn't feeling it. Something was missing. That something was Betty. This was the first time in his life she was not with him and he was lost without her.

Suck it up, he said to himself as he boarded the plane back to Philadelphia and his beloved Betty. He had to get over this feeling of loss just because she was not there. When he walked through the door, Betty ran and jumped into his arms and kissed him so hard she broke the skin on her bottom lip. This was the first time in their lives they had been apart, and those three days seemed like three years.

As she pulled Richard to their room she practically tore off his clothes, and he returned the favor. They typically were respectful about her mother's peace and quiet, but today, they forgot they weren't alone in the house. The time away from each other created such a cavernous void in their hearts, that passion and desire consumed both of them like a massive wall of fire.

After the flames of passion had subsided and the heat of desire had cooled, it was time for some real talk.

"So, what did you think of Miami?" Betty said as she pulled the sheet up over her breasts.

"It was nice like I thought it would be, but it didn't feel right for me," Richard said as he searched the room for his pants.

"So on to UCLA, right?"

"Yes, they're next." As Richard replied he fixed his eyes on Betty's reaction. "You don't want me to do any of this, do you?"

"Any of what?"

"Going to college and playing ball, that's what."

"That's your dream, Richard. Ever since we were kids that's all you've talked about."

"That's not all I've talked about, you are part of that dream too."

As a tear rolled down Betty's cheek she said, "I know that Richard, that's been not just your dream, but mine as well."

"So, what's the problem?"

Betty thought for a minute. This was the perfect opening to express her fears and concerns about her mother. *I can't leave my mother alone here in Philly and go to Miami or California, or where ever!*

"Who said you have to leave her? She can come with us wherever we go."

"No Richard, she is not that strong for all that travel, her heart is too weak."

He knew this was a subject she was not going to change her position on easily. He finished dressing and went downstairs to read more of the literature UCLA had sent him, and prepare for his visit to the city of angels.

***

The following week, Richard was headed to the Golden State to be a potential UCLA Bruin. The school's history included coach John Wooden, "The Wizard of Westwood," and legendary players like Kareem Abdul-Jabbar and Bill Walton.

The welcome wagon was out in full force and no enticement was spared, including women. Not just any women but Black, Caucasian, Asian, Latina, and various mixtures of all of them. It was a female rainbow!

Richard loved Betty deeply. He had loved her since the second grade and nothing had ever tested his love and commitment like what was before him. These women, beautiful as they were, had no chance at getting his heart for that belonged to Betty. His body? Now that was another question! He was exposed to something he had never been exposed to before, beautiful women who all seemed to want him.

In reality, these women didn't want him, they worked on the school's behalf to get him to sign with the school. They were there to show recruits a "good time." They were basically prostitutes. As one thing led to another, before he was aware of it, the unthinkable happened. Richard was unfaithful to Betty for the first time in their relationship. A relationship that spanned decades.

Guilt not only ate him up, it swallowed him completely, leaving him numb and in a zombie-like trance. How could he have been so weak to give in to temptation like that?

I'll just come clean with Betty and tell her the truth. Then he thought, *What if she doesn't handle it well, then what?*

With more questions than answers, Richard went home to Betty with a guilt-filled heart...and fear. He feared losing the only woman he has ever loved, and the fear of living life without her. When Richard walked through the door this time, Betty didn't run and jump into his arms. He didn't know how she knew, but he knew she did.

As he tried to kiss her, she turned her head and walked out of the room and upstairs to cry in solitude. After an hour or so, Richard mustered up enough courage to go and talk to her.

"I know I've messed up baby, I'm sorry, please, forgive me!" he said with tear-filled eyes and a quivering voice.

Strangely, Betty was composed."Yes, you messed up, not just for you, but for me too. Both our lives will forever be changed by what you've done. You will always feel a sense of guilt, and I'll always feel a sense of betrayal. So the trust factor is gone!."   Richard fell to his knees and pleaded. "Don't say that Betty, don't say that, that's the hurt and pain talking right now, in time we can get past this and put this behind us."

"No. I can't get past this. I still love you, but I don't trust you. And to me, if you don't have trust, you have nothing."

Walking halfway across the room, Betty turned and said, "Oh, by the way, you're going to be a father. That's why I'm not leaving you."

Betty was a product of divorced parents and made a promise to herself that she would never do that to her children. Richard picked himself off the floor and sat in a chair with his head in his hands. *I'm going to be a father.* Another thought entered his mind as well, this one not so pleasant. *What kind of household would it be for a child?"*

Betty still loved him, but she didn't trust him. There was a permanent coolness in her demeanor. They stayed together and had another child. But the marriage was never the same despite the fact that they put their broken hearts back together.

As far as basketball and UCLA...Richard blew out his knee and his hoop dreams were over.

The Crack in the Mirror

They continued to live in Betty's mother's house even after the death of Betty's mother.

Legally they were man and wife. In reality they had become distant strangers. The crack was just too deep to overcome.

CHAPTER 2
Earl & Linda

Siblings have a bond that is unbreakable and strong enough to withstand any test that bond might encounter. Such was the case of Earl and Linda. They had two loving parents who cared for them and raised them with a strong sense of family. Ever since Earl was a boy he was told by both their parents, "You look out for your little sister because you're the oldest."

One day at recess, Linda ran crying for Earl. A sixth grade girl had hit her. Linda was a forth grader and smaller than this girl who was in the same grade as Earl. When he saw his little sister crying and a slight blood trail on her lip, he went looking for the girl, and found her.

As he stood in front of her he asked, "Did you hit my little sister?"

Feeling cocky, the girl replied, "Yeah, I hit her, what are you going to do about it?"

Earl was confronted with a dilemma. His parents had always told him, "You don't hit girls." But their other words, "You look out for your little sister," were also in his head. He decided protecting Linda outweighted hitting a girl. He sent a right fist to her face and took Linda by the hand. As they left the playgound he wondered, *I did the right thing, didn't I? That's what mama and daddy always said, "Look out for your little sister."*

As the years progressed, the siblings were clearly different people in terms of character and life choices. Earl was more of a straight arrow, one might even say boring, with no desire for drama. Linda on the other hand, liked excitement and taking risks. Earl didn't get high, but Linda did. As a result, she hung around drug dealers who she claimed were "good people."

On one occasion, these "good people" got Linda high and raped her. It wasn't until many years later that Earl and his father found out about it the secret Linda and her mother had been keeping.

"Mama why didn't you tell me at the time about this?"

With her eyes welling up with tears, she said, "I knew what you would do and I didn't want you in prison for the rest of your life."

She was right. He would have been in prison because he would have gone looking for them, found them, and killed them. Their parents were from the South, and had definite ideas on what a boy could do and what a girl should do.

By standards today, I suppose you could say their parents were showing favoritism toward Earl. He did things and went places they did not allow their daugther to expereince.

Earl was older and he was a male. Their parents believed that men could do certain "things," and still be called, Mister. But. if a woman did those same things, she would be called a whore or slut. This dual set of rules for the siblings led to Linda harboring pent up negative feelings toward Earl. She didn't see, nor understand where her parents were coming from, no matter how they explained it.

"Linda, if Earl is falling down drunk in the middle of the street, do you know what people are going to call him?"

Linda sighed, and said in a not caring tone, "What Mama?"

Her mother put her hands on both her shoulders and said, "Mr. Franklin."

If you did that same thing, what do you think people would call you?"

Not really wanting to hear any of this, Linda said, "I don't know Mama, you tell me!"

Linda's mother took her hands off Linda's shoulders and said, "You better remember who you are talking too young lady, you hear me?"

"Yes, I hear you Mama. It's just that Earl gets to do everything and I can't do nothing."

"How many times do I and your father have to say this? Earl is a boy and he is older, there are things he can do and places he can go that you can't because you're a girl and younger."

Linda didn't hear a word her parents said in their attempt to protect her from the pitfalls that a young girl could fall victim too. Linda only saw her parents as restrictive, and most importantly, in her view, favoring Earl. It didn't matter that it wasn't true, because to her it was, and that's all that mattered. She acted in public and around Earl like she had love for her brother, but deep inside a resentment festered, and Earl was totally unaware.

***

His little sister went into adulthood carrying baggage from childhood about Earl being the "favorite" child. Their parents grew older and had health problems. When their father passed away their mother's health already had taken a turn for the worse. She had a series of strokes and no longer could care of herself. They were faced with the choice of putting their mother in a nursing home.

Their mother knew decisions had to be made too and she didn't want the nursing home to take her house in exchange for the cost of health care. She would have to sign her home over to Earl or Linda to prevent that. Since their mother had been staying with Linda, Earl agreed to put Linda's name on the house.

After they signed all the appropriate papers, Linda said, "If something happens to Mama, you know I'll be fair."

Earl smiled, hugged her, and said, "I'm not worried about that, I trust you, you're my sister." Earl wasn't worried about Linda doing the right thing because their mother made her wishes about the house very clear. She first wanted Earl to have it because he and his wife were living in an apartment and Linda had a house. When Linda got bent out of shape about that, their mother just wanted the house sold after her death and they would split the money from the sale.

***

Earl and Linda's mother fought her battle to beat her bad health as long as she could, but she wound up losing that fight. After the funeral and all the chaos had settled down, Earl went over to Linda's and asked about the house.

"So, what's happening with Mama's house?"

"What do you mean, what's happening with the house?" replied Linda as if Earl were speaking in a foreign language.

"I mean, is it on the market? Do you have it listed?" He was getting a little irritated by Linda's act.

"Why do you ask?" said Linda, turning and walking away.

Following her, Earl said, "I'm asking because you know, like I know, what Mama's wishes were regarding the house. I could use my half to help me get my own home."

"I don't know what you're talking about, Mama left the house to me, it's in my name."

"I know it's in *your* name Linda, we agreed to do that so the nursing home wouldn't take her house. So what are you saying?"

"What I'm *saying* is Mama left the house to *me* and that's why it's in my name." Earl looked at his sister in total disbelief. "You know that's not what Mama wanted, she had two children, not just one!"

Without blinking an eye Linda said, "If you want, you can have your old bedroom suite Mama had in one of the bedrooms."

Feeling the rage building and burning him like a hot poker, Earl looked Linda in the eye and said, "I will never set foot inside this house again." On the drive back to his apartment, he wondered, *How could she do this to me? I know she thinks I was the favorite, but this is hateful.*

Earl was more hurt than angry, money was only part of it. What hurt him more than anything was the fact that Linda valued money more than her brother, something Earl had a hard time coming to grips with. In the Bible, Judas betrayed Jesus for thirty pieces of silver. To Earl, this was no different! Linda loved money more than she loved him and that reality shook him to his core. The love he felt for Linda, thelittle sister his parents told him to always look out for, was dying and on life support, because of the mortal blow she had delivered to his heart.

For eight years, the two of them went without seeing or speaking to one another until...

One day Earl was reading an article about boxer Ruben "The Hurricane" Carter who was falsely accused of murder and sent to prison. Upon his release, he was asked if he had any hatred for the people who put him in prison although he was innocent. The Hurricane said, "No, because hatred consumes the vessel that holds it".

When Earl read that he thought, "Wow! That's really true. Because the object of your hatred doesn't feel a thing, you are the one suffering by carrying all that negativity."

Having that epiphany, Earl decided he had to forgive Linda—not for her, but for himself, so he could move forward in his life without the burden of hatred and pain. Earl and Linda started seeing and talking to one another and Earl did what he swore he would never do, go over to Linda's house. They were speaking, even laughing together, but things were awkward between them as far as Earl was concerned. He never brought up the situation with their mother's house.

Linda couldn't help but feel the coolness in Earl. She lamented to Earl's wife,   "When I hug him and say I love you, he doesn't say it back."

Earl couldn't say, "I love you", because Linda had killed that love eight years ago and there was no getting it back. After about three years of Earl's attempt at reconciliation he grew tired of pretending like everything was fine.

Earl felt clearing the air when you have wronged someone, means someone has to admit that what they did was wrong. After admitting that wrong, you ask for forgiveness from the person you have wronged. To him, Linda never admitted she was wrong in how she treated him. To her, she was justified in her actions.

Earl went over to Linda's to get things out in the open about how he felt. What he really wanted was for Linda to just admit she was wrong and say she was sorry; he knew the money was long gone. Having his sister apologize meant more to him than any amount of money.

"Hey," Linda said as she opened the front door to let Earl in. "What's up?"

Earl felt he already knew what was going to happen when he said what was on his heart. "There is something we need to address once and for all," he said as he scooted closer to Linda on the sofa.

"What's that?" Linda asked puzzled.

"You and me and what happened with Mama's house," replied Earl.

Linda was automatically defensive and uncomfortable. "Mama left the house to me!" she exclaimed, as if to convince herself of what she had just said.

"You know what you did was wrong and so does anyone who knows about our situation."

"I don't care what anybody else thinks, that's my Mama, not theirs!"

"You're forgetting one thing Linda, she was my mother too, not just yours! After all these years, you still don't see where you are wrong, do you?" said Earl in a soft voice.

He didn't raise his voice because he knew that would be her stance. He also knew this would be the last time he would visit her.

The love was dead for his sister, not because he wanted it that way, but because that's the way she made it. This crack was just too big to overcome.

The Crack in the Mirror

What the mother wanted was not what Linda wanted. Family can cause you to be blind when it comes to business matters because you want to trust family; no lawyers needed.

Family can make you take your guard down and leave your heart wide open to take a hit you never saw coming.

CHAPTER 3
Rick & Brian

To say Rick and Brian were best friends is an understatement. They were more like brothers. Not only did they grow up next door to each other, they were even born in the same hospital, two days apart. As children they made a pact: "You for me and me for you, today, tomorrow, forever!" They shared everything with each other from candy to clothes, and when they got older it changed to cars and girls.

During their senior year in high school all kinds of thoughts about the future swirled around in their heads. Then she walked in. As the two of them were in study hall looking at brochures from different colleges and universities, Veronica walked by. She was statuesque with skin the color of midnight and the texture of creamy butter. Her lips were succulent like rose petals after the rain. Both of them stopped in mid-sentence and as she made her way to her desk and thought, *She's beautiful.*

She was an Army brat and her father had been transferred to Fort Benning there in Georgia. She was only there to complete the one semester she needed to graduate. The two of them were so smitten with her that they didn't even hear the lunch bell ring. It wasn't until they heard the other students begin to leave the room that they snapped out of their trance.

"Did you see her!" Brian said with his mouth still open.

"Yeah, I saw her B-man" said Rick, remembering to breathe.

Brian stood up and watched Veronica walk toward the cafeteria, following every movement of her ample hips as she swayed. "I got to find out who she is."

Though they were best friends, Rick and Brian were individuals. Brian was more assertive and outgoing than Rick who was somewhat shy and sensitive, especially with the ladies. Brian referred to women as Ho's, while Rick detested that word in regards to his African American sisters. Brian was his boy so he tolerated him using it, but he didn't like it.

True to form, Brian was on it. He spotted her in line getting her lunch, and in his smooth I-want-to-get-with-you voice said, "I don't believe I've seen you before, are you new here?"

Being an Army brat, Veronica had been to many different countries and U.S. cities, so she knew a line when she heard it. "Yes, I'm new here" she replied, waiting to see what else Brian was going to say.

"My name is Brian," he said as he extended his hand to shake hers.

"It's nice to meet you Brian, my name is Veronica." She smiled through perfect teeth framed by her shoulder-length black hair."See you around," she said as she turned and continued to pay for her lunch.

Brian ran back to Rick to give him the scoop on the new girl.

"Her name is Ver-on-i-ca!" Brian said stressing each syllable with a smile.

What a beautiful name for a beautiful girl, Rick thought to himself.

***

After school the friends saw Veronica standing by a bench near the bus stop.   "Are you waiting for someone?" Brian inquired as his eyes drank her like she was a tall glass of water.

"Yes, I am. I'm waiting for my father." As the three of them stood in awkward silence, Veronica asked, "Are you going to introduce me to your friend?"

Forgetting Rick was even there, Brian said, "My bad, this is my best friend in the world Rick. Rick, this is Veronica."

"It's nice to meet you Best Friend in the World Rick," Veronica said with a little laugh.

Rick was spellbound. He wasn't like Brian who didn't know the meaning of the word unsure. "It's a pleasure to meet you Veronica," he said as he put out his hand to shake hers. When she touched his hand, he felt a sensation that interrupted his breathing momentarily. It was so slight that only he knew it.

Just then, her father pulled up and she got in the car. "See you guys tomorrow!" she said as she leaned out the window as the car sped away.

Brian was clearly in lust, while Rick was feeling more than just a physical attraction. As they walked home the two of them knew the other was interested in Veronica. It was awkward, so they talked about everything but her.

***

The next day they both learned she shared a class with each of them. Each wondered, was this going to be a good thing or a bad thing?

Weeks went by and Veronica had established a friendship with each of the best friends, but one friendship began to change into something else. Veronica told Rick and Brian about how she had bounced around from army base to army base all her life, never really having a place to call home. This was the last stop for her father who was retiring after her high school graduation.

She confessed that she never got close to people because of her constant moving. Knowing she could now give in to her feelings—if some were there—she let her emotional guard down and let her heart lead her. Where it took her was to Rick!

All their young lives, Brian always got the girls he wanted. He was good looking, athletic, and he could charm the fuzz off of a peach by just looking at it with his green eyes. He loved the ladies and the ladies loved him...and he knew it. Rick was reserved, quiet, in the background mostly, and barely noticed. He wasn't a jock, he wasn't ugly, but he was no Adonis; just a nice-looking guy with a good heart.

Brian's persona was so large that Rick felt like he was always walking in Brian's shadow, and that was why he settled for the girls Brian didn't want. This time, the girl they both wanted, had eyes for Rick. And more importantly, Rick had her heart.   As time went on and senior year was quickly approaching, the friends began to argue more and more. This had never happened before in all the years they have known each other. Veronica could see their relationship was deteriorating and she felt responsible and powerless at the same time. She knew she was the wedge driven between them. She felt powerless because she could do nothing to stop the eroding of the friendship. She had feelings for Rick, and for the first time in her life, she was not going to let him go, no matter what!

***

Three days before graduation, Veronica decided it was time to stop this emotional roller coaster once and for all. She asked Rick and Brian to meet her in the park to clear the air. Rick agreed. Brian did not.

"Say what you got to say right now," Brian yelled as they stood outside the school auditorium before graduation practice.

"Here at school isn't the best of places for a conversation like this Brian," Veronica said.

"Why not? This is where it all started!"

"OK! Since you want to force the issue Brian, fine!" Veronica snapped. I've liked you and Rick since the first day I met the both of you, and I know how the two of you feel about me."

"So, what are you getting at?" Brian blurted in his typical blunt fashion.

"What I'm getting at, as you put it Brian, is I have to make a decision that is going to cause one of you pain and I don't want to do that."

Rick stood in silence as he focused on his fellow classmates as they prepared the auditorium for the graduation ceremony.

"Just say what you got to say Veronica and drop all the drama," Brian said through clenched teeth.

"You're already getting ugly and I haven't even finished what I'm going to say!"   "Let me finish it for you baby," said Brian with anger in his voice. "You're in love with Rick, aren't you?"

Rick snapped out of his trance, "What! In love with me? What are you talking about? Is that true, is that why you wanted to have this talk?"

"Yes Rick, I'm in love with you. I didn't plan on it and I wasn't looking for it, it just happened."

Brian took a step back and looked at Rick and then at Veronica.

"Best friend in the world, right?" Brian said smurking at Rick.

Brian stormed off calling Rick and Veronica everything but their names.

"Wait, Brian, B-Man, come back!"

As Rick and Veronica stood in silence, a tear rolled down Veronica's cheek. Rick embraced her as he had longed to do since the first day he saw her. He gently kissed her rich moist lips that tasted more pleasurable than he imagined.

"What now?" Vernonica asked as they gazed into one another's eyes.

Rick wrinkled his brow, "I don't know. I'd like things to be like they've always been, but I honestly don't know if they can be. As far as I'm concerned, he has been —and still is, my best friend."

"Just give him some time. We have a future to plan my love."

***

After graduation new chapters of their lives were being written, but Brian held on to old paragraphs. For the first time in his womanizing life, he was in love with a woman who was not in love with him. And to top it off, the man she was in love with was his best friend! It was a bitter pill to swallow, especially for him, because he had never been told no, by any woman.

Rick and Veronica went on to college there in Atlanta; he to Morehouse, she to Spelman, so they could be close to each other. After college graduation they were married.

Brian had refused to speak to Rick after that day outside the auditorium in high school. They missed one another, but Brian's pride never allowed him to mend his friendship. Through it all, Rick loved his friend. Two years after Veronica and Rick married they had a son; a little boy. Guess what they named him? Brian Marcus...after the "B-Man" as Rick used to call him.

***

As Rick and Veronica planned their ten-year anniversary, Veronica wanted to invite Brian to the celebration.

"What do you think about inviting your old friend to the party?"

"I would love to see him because I still love him as my brother," Rick said as he smiled at memories of the fun they used to have together in the old neighborhood.

"OK, it's settled. I'll send him the invitation. Do you think he will come?"

"I don't know. But I hope he does."

"Well Rick, all you can do is extend the invitation and see if it's accepted, like when you extended your hand to me when we first met." Laughing, Rick hugged her and told her he loved her for that."

Every RSVP was returned, except Brian's.

Many friends from Rick's old neighborhood were there and they all were asking, "Where is Brian?" As things began to wind down and the guest began to leave, Rick and Veronica turned and saw Brian.

"You thought I wasn't coming, didn't you?" Brian said as he sipped his drink.

"Yeah, I did, think that," said Rick who saw how the years had not been kindly to his old friend. Brian put his drink down and said, "I came for one reason, to look you in the eye and see if I could still call you best friend."

Looking at him Rick said, "Well, what did you decide?"

Picking up his drink and finishing it with one big swallow, Brian said, "I can't do it." He turned and walked away, ignoring Veronica's plea to come back.

The Crack in the Mirror

The hurt and pain between the former best friends was too much to overcome; they both knew it. Brian felt Rick had betrayed him and his anger continued to smolder more than fifteen years later.

The best friends were no more. They had gotten to a place of civility with one another, but things would never be the same. That ship had sailed and ran aground on a crack too big to move beyond.

CHAPTER 4
Blake & Cindy

The relationship of father and daughter is special. Fathers love their sons, but daughters hold a place in father's hearts that can't be touched by anyone but them. Such was the relationship Blake had with his daughter Cindy, who he called his Shining Star. Blake loved Cindy more than life itself and there was nothing he wouldn't do to make her happy, well, almost nothing. Blake was drawn to the streets of Detroit like a moth to a flame...and you know what happens to a moth when he gets too close to the flame!

Because of his love of the streets, Cindy's mother Carrie, and Blake didn't see eye to eye. The one thing they could agree upon was Cindy's happiness and well being; they just had different opinions on how to achieve it. Cindy's mother was a physician's assistant for a prominent doctor in the city. Blake? He was a hustler. That's all he knew and he didn't want to know anything else. As far as he was concerned, "I hustle because I'm good at it."

Blake could have done other things, but the lure of the streets was just too great, and the freedom it afforded him had him hooked. He often would tell Carrie, "I don't know how you work a 9 to 5; that would drive me crazy!"

Carrie would always counter, "How does doing 9 to 20, sound? Would that drive you crazy?" That would usually end that conversation.

There is one thing about the streets, you may run them and think you are controlling them, but in the end, they always win. You wind up dead or in prison; those are the choices. Blake found that out the hard way when he got busted for possession of cocaine with the intent to deliver. As you would imagine, he went away to prison, sentenced to 15 to 30 for his drug bust.

That was bad for sure, but what was killing him inside was he would be out of Cindy's life for a long time. When he went to prison she was 7 years old. If he did just the minimum of his sentence she would be a grown woman when he got out. Blake did his time and he got out early for good behavior—twelve years later. But it seemed like more than one hundred and twelve years because he was away from his Shining Star.

The bus ride from the state penitentiary took Blake to the bus depot in downtown Detroit. As he stepped off the bus, he wondered how Cindy would react to him after all these years? Would it be like they never missed a beat? Or would it be awkward, like two strangers meeting for the first time? He hailed a cab and headed over to the address his wife and daughter now lived. His release would be a surprise to Cindy.

Cindy never saw Blake in prison because as he told Carrie, "I don't want my daughter to see me in a cage like an animal." Cindy had no contact whatsoever with her father for all those years and it made her bitter toward him. In her mind he may have loved her, but he loved the streets more, and she hated him for that.

As the cab pulled up to the house, Blake felt a sense of fear. He had lived with killers, rapists and thieves, but hadn't felt this kind of fear. He had second thoughts as to if this was a good idea or not.

Well, only one way to find out, he said to himself. With shaky legs and a heart pounding as hard as a drum, he climbed the stairs.

When he rang the doorbell Carrie answered. She just starred at him. He broke the silence, "You look good Carrie"

"You just been in prison too long, everything is going to look good to you!" Carrie said with a smile. She gave him a tight squeeze and invited him in.

"Where is she?" Blake asked, drying his sweaty palms on the sides of his pants. "She's upstairs taking a bath and changing out of her work clothes; I'll call her down. Cindy, are you almost done up there?" Carrie turned to Blake and said, "She is slow at getting ready just like you, always primping."

"I don't know what you mean?" said Blake, with a half-smile.

"You know, just like I know, you couldn't pass a mirror without stopping to look and primp, Blake Roberts!" They looked at each other and burst into laughter. As their laughter faded Cindy came down the stairs. She was no longer that little girl he left so many years ago. She had become a beautiful young woman who was descending like an angel from heaven.

Halfway down the stairs, Cindy stopped. "When did you get out?"

"I got out this morning Honey," Blake said with a dry mouth.

"That's nice," Cindy said as she reached the final landing and walked past him.

"That's all you got to say? 'That's nice?'" said Blake, hurt and confused.

"What do you want me to say? I'm glad you are home Daddy! I really missed you Daddy! Is that what you want to hear?" said Cindy with cold attitude.

Carrie got nose to nose with Cindy and said, "Your father has made some bad choices in life and he has gone to prison for those choices. But understand this, he is still your father!"

Not wanting the situation to become anymore heated than it was, Blake stepped in between them.

"She is not a little girl anymore Carrie," Blake said, hurt but understanding his daughter's pain. "If she's got something to say, say it!"

Carrie backed off and let things play out.

"Well? Is there something on your mind Cindy?"

"You going to try to play daddy now just because you out? It's a little too late for that now if you haven't noticed!"

"I would like for us to get back that closeness we once had Cindy, remember?"

Through the tears running down her cheeks that hugged her chin, Cindy said, "I'm not 7 years old anymore Dad. The Cindy you knew doesn't exist!"

Holding her hands in his, Blake said, "I know yesterday is gone, but today is here and tomorrow is on the way. I'm concerned about the present and the future, not the past. The past is gone, we can't do anything about it, but we can do something about here and now and the future."

Cindy pulled away from her father and screamed, "Do you think you can just walk back into my life after all these years and we can be like we were?"

Blake sat her down and said, "No sweetheart, I don't think that. Twelve years changes people; neither of us is the same person we were twelve years ago. Just give us a chance to try to get it back," Blake hung his head with a heavy sigh.

"I need some air," Cindy said as she raced around the house to find her keys and snatched her jacket from the hook near the door.

Blake didn't know what to say. He didn't want to be too forceful, and at the same time he wanted to grab his baby girl and hug the pain away. He chose to just sit back in the chair and let her go. After Cindy stormed out of the house and peeled out of the driveway, Carrie and Blake just shook their heads.

"What do you think Carrie?"

"This is happening so fast," Carrie said, trying to console the father of her child who had been gone for more than a decade. She had hurt feelings too, but they would have to stay on the back burner until Cindy's emotions were dealt with. "For Cindy right now, she had a dad for seven years, then she doesn't have a dad for twelve years, then she has a dad again. It's a adjustment for her."

"You're right as usual Carrie. I need to give her some space and time to soak this all in I suppose. Tell her I'll be in touch with her and this is where I'll be; and here is the phone number she can reach me at if she wants to."

"Do you need a ride somewhere?"

"No, I'm going to walk to my sister's house, she doesn't live far from here. I need to think about some things." Blake reached for the door. Part of his early release agreement was that he had to stay with his sister, since he and Carrie were divorced three years after his conviction. Also, he had to be employed and that could be a major problem as ex-cons weren't exactly at the top of any employer's lists. Blake wasn't sure what to expect from Cindy, but the reception he received from her was not the one he expected. This was going to take some work to fix.

***

As the sounds of the city played an urban symphony in his ears, Blake thought, *I don't know if I can get my daughter back, but I've got to try.*

When he arrived at his sister's house she yelled, "BLAKE!" She was so loud that the people on the street turned to see what the fuss was all about.

"Hey Sis!" Blake said in response to her loud welcome.

"You better get over here and hug me boy!" she said with extended arms. "It's so good to have you home Blaze, I've missed you so much."

Darla had given her little brother the nickname, Blaze because he once was an outstanding sprinter on the high school track team. He had been offered a scholarship to the University of Michigan, but as with anything positive in his life, the pull of the streets was just too strong for him to resist.

"I've missed you too "D. And I appreciate you letting me stay with you."

"Shut up fool! You're my baby brother, I got you!" said Darla as she grabbed him and gave him a big squeeze again.

"So, what's up with you and Cindy? How did she react to you being out?"

Blake released Darla from his embrace, looked her in the eye and said, "Not well."

Darla's voice got soft and broken when she asked, "Wha-What do you mean, not well?"

Blake turned and they walked toward the kitchen to get a beer.

"I mean not well, as in, she couldn't care less if I'm out or not, that's what I mean!"

"Blaze, you got to give her some time, it's been twelve years. She's had to live without a father. She was a child when you left, now she's a young woman, do you understand?"

"I know she ain't a kid anymore, but she acted like I was nothing to her, just some dude on the street!"

Darla took the beer from Blake's hand, sat it on the table, looked him in the face, and said, "In many ways Blake, you *are* just some dude on the street to her, she doesn't know you anymore."

"I'M HER FATHER!" Blake screamed at the top of his lungs.

"I know you're upset Blake, but you have to give it some time and what will be, will be."

***

Blake took Darla's advice and didn't rush things with Cindy. He let her precede at her own pace, even though it was slow. On one of their times together, Blake bared his soul to Cindy.

"Cindy, I love you more than life itself, you know that, don't you?"

Cindy looked her father in the eye and asked, "Even more than the streets?"

While that remark cut Blake like a knife to his heart, he answered with a lump in his throat, "Yes baby, that was the old me, this is the new me; just give me a chance."

"A chance to do what? Hurt me again? Be second behind the hustle of the streets as to what is important to you?"

"I deserve that. My track record hasn't been too good in the past, but that's what I'm saying Cindy, the streets are in the past!"

As a tear rolled down her left cheek, Cindy said, "That may be true, maybe, but the hurt and pain I've felt all these years because the streets meant more to you than I did, is still here today, Father."

"Let me make it up to you Cindy, please don't cut me out of your life."

"You mean like the way you cut me out of your life?" Cindy said angrily.

"So now you're going to make the same stupid mistake I made and justify it with, You-did-it-so-I'm-doing-it-too! Is that right?" Blake took a deep breath. "You're angry with me for not being there when you were a child, a time when you really needed your father. I get that. But that was yesterday Baby. It's gone, and it's not coming back. You're angry with me for choosing the streets over you, I'm angry at me also for making that choice. I was not in a good place mentally and I made poor decisions during that time in my life.

"And that's not to offer up excuses, but it's simply a matter of fact. It boils down to this Cindy, do you want a relationship with your father or not? I can't change what happened in the past, but I can change what happens in the present and what happens in the future. All I can do his extend my hand. It's up to you to grab it, or not. It's your choice".

Having heard her father's emotional plea for a chance at a relationship with her, Cindy said, "No. That's my choice. Don't call me ever again and I won't call you either!"

The Crack in the Mirror

Cindy, like a lot of adult children, could not let the past go because of childhood hurts—perceived or real, that were committed by a parent. What children don't understand, not until they are parents, is just because you are a parent, doesn't mean you don't make mistakes and bad decisions.

Cindy's pain over her father's past choices was too much for her to handle. She still loved her father, but she was afraid to trust him again with her heart. The crack in her heart would not allow her to reestablish her relationship with her father.

CHAPTER 5
Norma & Tommy

An R&B group in the 1960's, called the *Intruders*, had some nice records (yeah, I said records) back in the day. One of these records was, "I'll always love my Mama," which goes without saying, right? The singers confess that a son's mother is his "favorite girl." That's how many sons view their mothers; they love them unconditionally unless, something drastic damages that love.

Norma and Dexter were a happy couple to all that came into their presence. Dexter, the handsome Marine captain, and Norma, the lovely, doting, military wife, were living the postcard of happiness. That's not to say being a career military man's wife was easy, because it wasn't. The constant relocating was hectic at times, but Norma made it work for her son, Tommy. When she married Dexter, she was well aware of what she was getting into; she too had been a military brat. Her father was a career Army man and she and her mother had been all over the world, from duty station to duty station.

Dexter received orders that said he was to deploy to Afghanistan in two weeks. Norma was troubled by the news. While she accepted the role of a military wife, she didn't like it at times like these. Tommy, upon hearing about his father would be stationed in Afghanistan, didn't take the news well.

"Why do you have to go Dad?" Tommy asked as his father began to pack.

Dexter stopped what he was doing and hugged Tommy. "Son, we've been over this many times before; it's my job to fight the bad guys in order to keep you and your mother safe."

To this 17-year-old boy, who understood the dangers of that part of the world, that answer didn't console him at all. Tommy hugged his father tightly as the ribbons on his father's chest dug into his own; he was now just as tall as his father.

"I know it's your job, and I know we've talked about this before, but it's so dangerous over there!" His father looked him in the eye and tried to comfort him. But he knew, not even adults could be comforted in times like these. It was too common to hear of the soldiers who were killed in combat. They all had known at least one military family who received the news that their loved one was killed in action.

"I'll be careful Son, don't worry about me. You have to be the man of the house while I'm gone, ok?"

This didn't make Tommy feel any better even though Dexter gave him assurances he would be safe. Norma heard the conversation between the two and didn't want to interrupt that father-son moment. She felt Dexter should know how Tommy felt about his father being placed in harm's way. She also felt Dexter needed to reassure his son and try to put his fears to rest about his safety.

This wasn't the first time Dexter was being sent overseas to some hostile area of the world, but he had never been sent to a place like Afghanistan. That's what made this deployment so different, and all concerned knew that. The two weeks flew by and   Dexter was on his way to where peace was a foreign concept.

Before he left, Norma being a military wife, didn't fill his head with, "I don't want you to go," "It's so dangerous over there!", or anything that could be a distraction to what must have been internally agonizing to him.

All she said was, "I love you and come back to me and Tommy." Being a career military man's wife, that's all she needed to say, because after all, she knew what she signed up for.

When Dexter arrived in Kabul, the first thing he did was let his family know he had gotten there safe and sound. They were so relieved to hear and see him on Skype that they both spoke over one another.

As the conversation ended, Tommy looked at his mother and wondered how she really was feeling?

When the conversation was over, Tommy said, "Mom, are you alright?"

Norma turned with a smile and a kiss for her little man on the cheek. "Yes son, I'm fine, get ready for bed, o.k.?"

"O.K. Mom," Tommy said as he made his way to his room.

In the silence of her bedroom, Norma thought things she couldn't share with her son; thoughts of what would she do if something happened to Dexter. How would Tommy handle it? These thoughts and many more, kept sleep away from her on this night and many more to come.

***

8 Weeks Later

Combat was heating up rapidly in Afghanistan as suicide bombings were becoming more frequent. All military personnel were instructed to use extreme caution when encountering civilian—men, women, AND children.

Dexter commanded a patrol that was out doing some reconnaissance in a village, when they came across two teenaged girls who couldn't have been any older than Tommy. As the girls approached with smiles and giggles, as teenage girls tend to do, they were given an order to stop. Acting like they didn't understand English, they continued moving closer to Dexter and his men. Once again, the command to stop was given, but this time in the language of the region, so Dexter knew they understood.

The two girls kept coming, laughing and giggling as they drew closer and closer to Dexter and his men. Seeing they were not going to stop after being warned twice, Dexter stood up to give the order to fire when a sniper's bullet hit him in the neck. His patrol opened fire killing the girls, who were meant to be a distraction for the sniper to kill an officer.

Three days later there was a knock at Norma's door. Two Marines stood in full Dress uniform. She didn't need to ask what did they want. She dropped to her knees. Her biggest fear had now become a frightening reality for her and Tommy.

Tommy, she thought, *What will I say when he comes home from school?* She was a military wife for sure, but she was a scared mother with a child who she had to tell his father was dead.

Feeling the weight of the world on her shoulders, she poured herself a drink from a bottle of scotch Dexter had in a kitchen drawer. She wasn't a drinker and didn't know you had to sip scotch, not drink it like water. After one gulp she began to choke and gasp for air. Once she regained her composure, she sat, and waited for Tommy.

He came through the door like he always did and headed straight through the living room to the kitchen. He didn't see his mom sitting in the chair holding her wedding picture and gripping a nearly full glass of scotch in the other hand.

"Hey Mom, we got any chips?" He didn't see her, but he knew she was in the house somewhere.

"Look over the sink Tommy." Her quivering voice sent alarm to her son who stopped rattling the chip bag and found her sitting on the couch.

"Mom, what's wrong?" he said as he looked at her with a glass of scotch. He knew she didn't drink.

Norma looked up with red, tear-filled eyes. "Your..."

Before she could finish her sentence Tommy screamed, "Don't say it! I don't want to hear it!" He ran to his room screaming, "No! No!"

Norma didn't know if she should go to Tommy or give him some space to digest what hadn't been said. Instead, she drank, and coughed. After a few more sips, she was able to handle it.

***

Dexter's body came home to a full military burial with honors. When the U.S. flag was draped over his casket Norma was drunk. Tommy was ashamed and embarrassed.

How could she disrespect my father's memory like that? he wondered.

Norma had to be helped into the limousine by Tommy and one of his dad's Marine buddies. When they made it home, Tommy held Norma by her shoulders, something he had never done before.

"What's wrong with you? Have you no respect for my father, your husband?"

She took off her coat and placed it on the chair. "What do you mean, what's wrong with me?" as she preceded to pour herself a drink.

"That's what I'm talking about, that right there! Your drinking Mom! You think you are the only one hurting?"

Norma took a sip from her glass and slurred, "I always knew this day could come, we all did, including your father. But until it comes, you don't know how you will handle it." Norma began to get angry at the judging eyes of her son.

"So, Thomas Michael Slone, you my daddy now?" Norma said as she sat her glass down on the table with force.

"No, I'm not your daddy, but you are not acting like my mother. And when I graduate next month, I'm out of here!" said Tommy as he stormed out the house.

"GO! See if I care!" screamed Norma as she continued to find the bottom of the scotch bottle. Tommy graduated and true to his word he left on the first thing smoking out of town, without even saying goodbye.

***

Years went by and Tommy met a nice girl, fell in love, got married and had a beautiful little girl. Norma and her scotch became one in the same. She no longer was drinking out of the bottle, the bottle was drinking out of her. Even though she wouldn't admit it— not even to herself, she missed Tommy. Not a day went by that she didn't think about him, or he about her. She had been his favorite girl... until she wasn't.

Death brings families closer together, or pushes them further apart. It depends on the strength of individual family members and if they are strong enough to deal with such a devastating blow as the death of a husband, or father? Norma was not strong enough to handle the loss of Dexter and sought strength and comfort from a scotch bottle. Tommy, who she was worried about, had more strength and courage than she did and dealt with his father's death.

Ten years after leaving home, Tommy found himself thinking about her more and more. He didn't know why she was on his mind so much, maybe something was wrong with her? He expressed his concerns to his wife who encouraged him to try to locate her.

Tommy wasn't sure he wanted to do that. The last words he heard from his mother were, "Go! See if I care!" As he dialed the last known number of his former home, he thought, *After ten years, what do I say? Hi Mom, how's things.*

Someone answered the phone, but it was not his mother."Hello, is Norma there?" he said in an unsure tone. "

Yes, she is, may I ask who is calling?"

Forgetting how to speak for a few seconds, he said, "It's Tommy, her son." As the words slid across his teeth, they sounded so foreign because they had not been spoken in so long.

"With whom am I speaking with? Tommy asked.

"This is her nurse, Mrs. Gates.""

Her nurse? What does she need a nurse for?" said Tommy in a cracking voice.

"I guess you don't know? Your mother has liver failure and not much longer to live, I'm sorry."

"When did all this happen?" asked Tommy as his wife saw the pained look on his face.

"She started having liver problems three years ago and it's gotten worst over the years," said Mrs. Gates.

"I see." Tommy slowly sat down on the couch. "Can she talk right now?"

"No, she can't at this moment because she's asleep after taking her pain medication, but I'll tell her you called"

"No, you don't have to tell her I called, I'll call back later."

"There may not be a later Tommy. Do you understand what I'm saying to you?"

"Yes, Mrs. Gates, I understand." Tommy hung up the phone. He had mixed emotions. She was gravely ill and his mother, but because of their estrangement, the love he had for her was waning at best. Was he a bad person for feeling this way? He talked it over with his wife Ellen, and as always, she knew just what to say.

"T-Baby, if you don't want to do it for you, do it for her."

"Ellen, why should I care what she wants? She didn't care what I wanted when she disrespected my father with her drunk ass! We don't even know if she wants to see me!" He paced the floor not knowing whether to cry or feel angry.

"As a mother, I know she wants to see her child, trust me." Ellen caught Tommy in the midst of his pacing, grabbed his face, and kissed his forehead. She left him to deal with his emotions as she went to prepare dinner.

***

A couple of days later Tommy called back. Norma answered. "I never thought I would hear your voice again Tommy, it's so good to hear from you."

"Yeah, it's good to hear your voice too Mom," he said in a search for what to say next.

"What made you call after all these years, Son?"

"You had been on my mind lately, so I thought I'd see what's going on with you."

"Well, I guess you see, huh?" Norma said in a weak whisper. "Come see me Tommy, before my eyes close for good."

His mother is dying. Tommy was ready to get off the phone. "I'll see Mom. Goodbye."

When he hung up the phone, Ellen was starring right through him.

"What?" Tommy asked in regards to the burning eyes of his wife.

"I'll see Mom? Is that all you got to say to your dying mother?" Ellen was furious.

"Yeah, I'll see," said Tommy as he disappeared down into his man cave.

***

After Ellen's constant insistence that he visit his mother, he gave in. Ellen could make him do what no other human being on earth could. With their child gripping their hands, they arrived to find Norma had been admitted to the hospital. She had taken a turn for the worst.

Children weren't usually allowed to visit patients on the critical care floor, but due to the circumstances, an exception was made. Norma was barely hanging on, but she wanted to see her son, his wife, and her granddaughter "before her eyes closed for the last time," as she put it. When the three of them entered the room, Ellen allowed Tommy a few moments alone with his mother.

"Hi, Mom," said Tommy without any emotion.

"Hello, Son, come closer," Norma said as she raised her hand to touch his face.

Tommy wanted to feel more, but the hurt was too deep.

"Who are those two beautiful ladies over there?" Norma asked, smiling toward Ellen and her granddaughter.

"Go ahead Sweetie, tell Grandma your name," Ellen said to her daughter as she nudged her toward the bedridden woman.

Norma sat up in bed as much as she could to greet the little angel.

"My name is Norma Diane Slone."

Norma began to cry uncontrollably, as did Tommy, but for different reasons. Norma's tears were for a son she never stopped loving, Tommy's tears were for a mother he wished he still loved.

The Crack in the Mirror

Norma slipped away soon after that, just like her son's love.
The crack between them never got a chance to be repaired.

CHAPTER 6
June & Alice

June and Alice shared the same likes and dislikes, mainly due to their parent's guidance. Their parents, Frank and Sharon, were college professors who constantly stressed the need for academic success. Though they shared many likes and goals, they were two different people with two different personalities.

Education was important to June. As for Alice, she had other hidden dreams. June wanted to be a college professor like her parents, travel the world on research projects, and see her name in educational journals and books. Alice was drawn to the bright lights of Hollywood with all its glitz, glamor, and everything that went with it. Yes, they were the same as far as their parents were concerned, but they really weren't.

As high school graduation approached, the question on both of their parent's minds was, where they would go to school?

During one of their "family meetings," their parents sat the girls down and asked, "What school have you decided on?" Frank hoped both girls would choose the University of Michigan where he and Sharon attended. If they didn't, that was okay, because this was about what the girls felt would be a good fit for them.

Alice, being the more out spoken of the two sisters answered, "I'm still considering three, but I'm close to narrowing it down to one, Dad."

Frank gave her that father-approving smile and said, "That's great Honey, because time is getting short and a decision is going to have to be made soon."

"I know Dad," Alice said smiling back at her father.

"What about you June? Have you made a decision on a school?"

"Yes, Dad, I'm going to Michigan, where you and Mom went," June said with a big grin.

"That's wonderful Baby!" Frank yelled as he looked at Sharon and thought, *At least I got one of them to go to Michigan.*

"That's good news girls. And Alice, don't wait too long on your decision, okay?" Alice smiled nervously and said, "I won't Dad."

Judgement day came—or least that's what it felt like to Alice, because she had to make a decision. If she was going to receive any financial aid and obtain student housing, she needed to get the paperwork going. Eventhough their parents were college professors, the girls still needed financial aid. Five years earlier,

Sharon fought and won a battle with breast cancer, however, the family finances took a huge hit. She had a rare form of breast cancer that was radical in the way it was attacking her body and a radical treatment was needed.

The treatments were not FDA approved, which meant they were not covered by insurance, which meant if you want it, you have to pay for it yourself. This wiped out all of the family savings, 401K's, and most of their stocks. This is why Frank was so concerned about the time table for the girls to make their college decisions.

June had already submitted her paperwork for her financial aid, housing, and tuition. She was all set to go to Ann Arbor. She knew what she wanted and she was not the kind of person to wait until the last minute to do things.

Alice, not so much. She really didn't want to go to college—Michigan or anywhere else. Her thoughts, hopes, and dreams were in Tinsel Town. Because of this, she hadn't made any choices about going to college because she wasn't really planning on going. Eventhough she knew in her heart of hearts college was not in her future, she didn't know how to tell her mother and father her true feelings. For her to do that would devastate them. Ever since she was a little girl all she heard them say was, "You are going to college."

So, yeah, it was judgement day for her, and then some. She couldn't put it off any longer. Alice decided to come clean with her parents and sister.

After she expressed her feelings of not wanting to go to college, her father said, "Alice, we've talked about not just June, but you too, going to college. Where is this coming from?"

Alice, seeing the hurt on his face and her mother's, said, "No Dad, you and Mom have talked about us going to college, it wasn't like it was an option!"

Frank was starting to get visibly upset and loud. "Excuse your mother and I for wanting you and your sister to have a decent life! An education is how you achieve that!"

Trying to bring down the heat in the room, Alice said, "Mom, Dad, you never once asked me, or for that matter June, what we wanted. It was always about what you wanted."

Sharon feeling stressed by the whole situation, said, "All your father and I wanted was just the best for you and your sister, can't you see that?"

Feeling like she needed to say something, June said, "We know that, Mom, and that's why we love you both."

Alice looked at June and thought, *What a suck up!*

Frank stood up and looked down on Alice. "Do you know what you want to do since college isn't what you want?"

Standing herself, Alice said in a confident voice, "I want to go out to Hollywood and be an actress."

Frank turned to Sharon and said, "Did you hear that Honey? Your daughter wants to go to Hollywood and be an actress." Frank turned back around to face Alice and burst into laughter and screamed, "ARE YOU CRAZY! YOU"VE LOST YOUR DAMN MIND GIRL!" Frank rarely would lose his temper, but when he did it wasn't pretty.

Sharon stood up and held Frank's face in her hands and said softly, "It will be alright Frank, calm down Baby."

Frank took Sharon's hands into his hands and said, "How can I calm down when Alice wants to throw her life away on some bullshit dream that she, and hundreds of other girls like her, come to see it turn into a nightmare?" "Do you know the odds of you becoming an actress Alice? I'll tell you, not very good!"

Having said all that Frank sat back down. He was mentally and physically drained by all that had transpired. June looked at her sister much more differently than she ever had before, it was like she was seeing her for the very first time. She was hurt that her parents were hurt, but what hurt most was Alice didn't think enough about their sibling bond to share with her the true feelings she kept inside.

As June was trying to make sense of what had just happened, Alice asked her, "Do you have anything you want to say to me? Let's just get it all on the table June."

"Yeah, I got something to say. You know how much Mom and Dad struggled behind Mom getting sick and the sacrifices Dad had to make to feed us, and keep a roof over our heads, don't you?"

"Yes, I know all of that June, so what's your point?"

"My point is, I think you are a selfish bitch!"

"JUNE!!" yelled Sharon and Frank almost at the same time. "You don't talk to your sister that way!"

"I apologize Mom and Dad for disrespecting you by cursing in your presence, but I do not apologize for saying what I said to her."

June left the room. Frank and Sharon hugged as Sharon cried on Frank's shoulder.

"Well, I guess that's my cue to exit stage right, as they say in Hollywood," said Alice.

"You think this is funny young lady? You've broken my heart, shattered your mother's dreams, and put a wedge between you and your sister!"

Wiping away tears, Alice said, "You speak of your broken heart, what about my heart that's broken too? You said I shattered Mom's dreams. What about neither one of you asking me what my dreams even were?"

June reentered the room to get her purse, and Alice said, "As far as there being a wedge between my sister and I, that's up to her, I still love her, as far as I'm concerned nothing has changed."

Hearing Alice's words, June walked toward the door and paused. She turned and looked at Alice, then turned back around and continued out the door.

"I guess that was pretty obvious how she feels wasn't it," sobbed Alice. "Everybody wants me to be what they want me to be. Nobody cares what I want! And because I dare to want to be something other than what all of you think I should be, I'm what now? Oh, a selfish bitch!

"Thanks for the love and support family!" Alice gathered her coat and keys and left her parent's house. She wasn't sure if she would see them, or June again in light of what just happened.

Later that night, Frank complained to Sharon that he was having trouble breathing, so she called an ambulance. By the time the ambulance arrived at the hospital, Frank had died from a massive heart attack. Because it was so sudden and no prior heart problems or family history of heart disease, his passing was quite puzzling to doctors.

As a result of so many questions and no answers, doctors asked Sharon was there anything going on in Frank's life that was causing him undue stress? Sharon was hesitant to say what first popped into her mind, but she knew in order for the doctors to get a clear picture as to the cause of Frank's death, she had to be completely honest.

Sharon looked at the doctors and said, "Early that day we had a family crisis that was emotionally stressful on all of us."

One doctor said, "I see, do you mind sharing with us the nature of that crisis?"

Sharon went on to tell the whole story of the events of the past day. Then she remembered Frank being short of breath when he was talking to Alice. She didn't think much about it at the time, but now she was wondering, was he in the beginning stages of having a heart attack then?

Not wanting to blame Alice for what happened, she was reluctant to ask her next question, "Is it possible that the argument Frank had with my daughter could have brought this on?"

The two doctors looked at each other and the head Cardiologist said, "Anything is possible. I'm not saying your daughter caused your husband's heart attack, what I'm saying is, anything is possible, Okay?"

June was in the room with her mother and she knew whose fault it was for her father's death, as far as she was concerned. "You know it's Alice's fault that Dad is dead don't you Mom?" said June as they walked out of the hospital.

Sharon took her hand as they walked to the parking lot and said, "Honey you can't say that for sure, we just don't know."

"Maybe you don't know, but I do! And I'll never forgive her for that, NEVER!"

At the funeral, it was a tense and stressful situation as these things often are. But this was on another level. What happened between Alice and Frank had gotten around to the whole family and had created divisions among other family members. Half of the family believed Alice was wrong for not wanting to go to college like her parents wanted her too. The other half thought Frank and Sharon should have let the girls make their own decision about what they wanted to do with their lives.

One person who was clear on how she felt was June. She left no doubt about her feelings. Both girls loved their father, but June, being the baby, worshiped the ground her father walked on. That's why her pain was so great and the loathing of her sister for killing him—as she saw it—was so immense.

The Crack in the Mirror

When the funeral was over, Alice caught a plane for Los Angeles and June packed up for Ann Arbor. The bond June thought she had with her sister was never really there. It was a mirage.

The permanent crack that was now between them, however, was quite real.

CHAPTER 7
The Bensons & The Longs

Moving to a new city is never easy. You're not familiar with the area, you know nothing about the doctors, or the school system. More of a concern for most people, is what kind of neighbors will I have? These thoughts were racing inside the head of Mary Benson as her husband Dave, drove them and their two children to their new home.

They had lived in Blue Island, Illinois for ten years, but Dave's job was downsizing so he had to relocate to another plant or be let go. Given the choice of really no choice, Dave packed up his family and headed west to Denver, Colorado, where he would be the new plant manager for Textron. While Mary had her own personal concerns she was silently contemplating, Dave had some of his own as well.

Denver was not Blue Island, it was a bigger city, things would be more spread out. He realized there were more people, which means more crime. Would his family be happy? Would they be safe? These were the thoughts that occupied Dave and Mary's minds as they traveled along the highway as it wound and twisted its way through the mountains.

Once they arrived in Denver, Mary was quite taken at how beautiful the landscape was as the Rockies stood in the background like majestic giants. The kids, Dave Jr. (or DJ as he was called), and Patty, jumped out of the car and began to explore their new backyard. Running from DJ, Patty wasn't paying attention to where she was going and she ran into the neighbors who were coming out of their house.

She stopped abruptly and looked up at the woman who said, "Well, hello there, what's your name?"

Patty, startled by the stranger, turned and ran toward DJ; they both ran to their parents.

"What's wrong?" Dave asked.

Catching his breath, DJ said, "There's people around back!"

Hearing that, Dave and Mary went to see what people the children were talking about. Dave and Mary turned the corner and saw what the children were talking about, standing there were the new neighbors, Cyrus and Karen Long.

After a few seconds of silence, Cyrus walked over to Dave and Mary and the kids.

"Hello neighbors, we're the Longs. I'm Cyrus, but you can call me Cy. And this is my wife Karen."

Feeling more at ease, Dave extended his hand and shook Cy's. "It's nice to meet both of you, we're the Bensons; my name is Dave, this is my wife Mary and our two children, DJ and Patty.

"I'm sorry, but we have to run, we've got an appointment we have to get too," said Cy as he opened the car door for Karen. "I know how it is moving into a new house, there's a thousand and one things to do. We'll give you a few days to settle in," said Cy as he got into the car. "Welcome to the neighborhood!!" he yelled as he pulled out of the driveway.

Mary turned to Dave and said, "What do you think about our new neighbors?"

Dave looked at DJ and Patty playing in the yard and said, "I think we're going to be happy here. I've got a good feeling about Cy and Karen."

"Me too," Mary said as she kissed Dave on the cheek.

***

A week and many unpacked boxes later, Dave and Mary decided to have Cy and Karen over for dinner. It was summer and the mountain air smelled fresh and clean. Technically, they were in Denver, but they really lived in a suburb of Denver called Centennial. Mary had most of the house together, but there were still a few things left to be done. She had at least made it comfortable for her family.

Dave thought it would be a good idea to put some steaks on the grill and have Mary make her "world-famous" macaroni salad, along with a lemon pound cake. That sounded good to him, plus some hot dogs for the kids. Cy and Karen came over with a bottle of wine that was a good vintage, and the evening went well.

Later in the evening, Mary asked Karen if she would like to come with her to put the kids to bed.

"I'd love too!" Karen said. She had always wanted children, but she couldn't have any of her own due to a car accident decades earlier that had damaged her ovaries. She had so much internal damage, they had to be removed and so was her opportunity to have children. Anytime she was around children, she was happy, and sad. It was a bittersweet situation, one she couldn't rectify, no matter how hard she tried.

As Mary and Karen went into the house, Dave and Cy talked. "How long have you two been here?" said Dave as he sipped on his second glass of wine.

"We've been here going on eight years now," said Cy, putting his feet up on a stool. "What brings you here?"

"My job is downsizing and I had to relocate here or find another job," Dave said in a I-didn't-have-much-of-a-choice tone. Cy took a drink of his beer and said, "Well, I can understand that, you do what you got to do for your family. Was

Mary okay with this?"

Dave paused and said, "At first, no, she wasn't. Everybody and everything she knew was in Blue Island, Illinois; that's where we lived for ten years.

"That's tough pulling up roots you've put down in a place and having to re-establish yourself all over again"

"Yeah, tell me about it."

Mary and Karen had now made their way back to the patio and Karen looked at Cy and said, "It's late honey, I think we should be heading home."

"Yeah, you're right, it is getting late and we should be going. Thanks for the dinner Dave and Mary, next time dinner is at our house."

Dave and Mary stood there with Dave's arm around Mary and Dave said, "That's a date, goodnight!" As Dave checked to make sure the coals were out from the grill and Mary clearned the table, he said, "I really like Cy, he's easy to talk too."

"I know what you mean, Karen is the same way, I think I've found my new best friend!"

"See honey, I told you we were going to be happy here."

***

On Dave's first day on the job as the new Denver Plant Manager of Textron he was nervous. He didn't know why; afterall, he had been a plant manager for the past ten years in Blue Island.

Oh well, he thought, *it's just first day on the job jitters, it will pass.*

Sure enough, the nervousness passed and upper management began to see what they had in Dave. He cared that the plant was clean, efficient, and producing a quality product. More importantly, he cared about the people who worked at the plant. While the job was a breeze, tensions with his neighbors began to heat up.

One day, Patty left her bike in the Long's driveway and Cy had to get out of his car to move it. He had a fit as he cussed and stomped up the walkway to the house.

Seeing this from the living room window, Mary called Patty. "Patty why did you leave your bike in Mr. Long's driveway?"

Sensing she was in trouble, Patty spoke with tear-filled eyes. "I'm sorry Mama, I won't do it again"

"Okay Honey, but you've got to tell Mr. Long you're sorry and that you won't do it again."

"Do I have too?"

"Yes, you have too," Mary said as she gave her daughter a hug. "Come on let's go."

With Patty in tow, Mary knocked on the door and Karen answered. "Hi Ladies, what brings you over?"

"Hi Karen, is Cy available? Patty has something she would like to say to him."

"Oh, okay, I'll get him, come in and have a seat."

When Cy entered the room his whole face changed. *Where was that friendly, happy-go-lucky guy she met just a few months ago?* Mary thought to herself.

"You got something you want to say to me?" said Cy as he sat down. "I don't, but Patty does. Go ahead Patty, tell Mr. Long what you came here to tell him." Mary motioned to Patty to stand.

"I'm sorry Mr. Long, for leaving my bike in your driveway, it won't happen again."

"It damn well better not happen again, because if it does, I'm not getting out of my car and move it. I'm just going to run over it, you got it!"

Patty was so scared she buried her face in her mother's lap along with her tears. Karen was frozen in disbelief.

"How dare you talk to a child, my child, that way after she had the courage to come over here to apologize for leaving her bike in your driveway!" screamed Mary. "Let's go Patty, we won't be back over here again!" Mary walked so fast that Patty couldn't keep up.

When Dave got home Mary told him the whole story, every sordid detail of what happened with the bike, and Cy's rant to Patty.

Dave was furious, "Does he not understand she is a little girl? Yes, she's wrong to have left her bike in his driveway, but she's a little girl!"

"Dave, I don't want you doing anything stupid, okay?" said Mary with a shaky voice.

"I'm fine Mary, I'm going to do what I feel I must do."

"What is that Dave?

"I'm putting up a fence between our properties."

"A fence? Are you sure about that, Dave?"

"You know the old saying, 'Good fences make for good neighbors.'"

"I thought we had good neighbors without a fence," Mary said as she went out and sat on the patio.

***

As time went on, the families remained cool toward one another. Dave and Cy just stopped talking to each other altogether. Now that the fence was up, they didn't even have to see each other. Karen and Mary missed the way things used to be. Karen didn't have many friends because she didn't have the bond of parenthood to share with many other women. She didn't allow herself to get close to people because of that void. In Mary, she found someone who she could feel comfortable with and she hated to lose that.

Mary thought of Karen as her sister, since she was an only child and had never had anything close to a sibling relationship. The two women felt the loss of the relationship openly, while the men hid the fact that it hurt them as well.

***

15 Years Later

Patty was now a beautiful young lady who was engaged to be married. Dave and Mary were so proud. Mary sent out invitations to family and friends from Blue Island, and she was excited. The ceremony was beautiful and Patty was a vision of loveliness as she walked down the aisle with her father on her arm. The reception was one big party and everyone was having a good time.

Cy and Karen walked in, uninvited! Dave made his way toward them and yelled, "What the hell are you two doing here!"

By then, Mary walked up and smiled at Karen. Their eyes spoke to the fact that they missed one another.

"Well, what are you doing here Cy?" Dave asked again.

"Over these past fifteen years, I've done a lot of thinking about our relationship as neighbors. I overreacted about Patty and the bike."

Dave took a deep breath. "Are you telling me, it has taken you this long to realize you overreacted to my little girl leaving her bike in your driveway? Is that what you're telling me Cy?"

Patty and her new husband had saw the commotion and came over to stand beside her father.

"What a surprise to see you Mr. and Mrs. Long after all these years," Patty said, now old enough to speak for herself. "We have lived next door to one another, but we may as well have lived in the next county. Mr. Long, I don't think you understand how much you hurt me. I was a child and you cursed and screamed at me."

Patty wiped away some tears and continued. "You not only hurt me, you made my father so mad that he almost did something that would have put him in prison had he done what he wanted to do."

Mary put her arm around Patty. "My mother is the only reason my father didn't do something to you, do you understand that?" Karen was crying, Mary was crying, DJ was just biting his lip, and Dave was just staring at Cy.

"I know Dave was upset with me for treating you like I did and I'm sorry for that Patty. I came here today to beg your forgiveness and your parent's forgiveness as well."

Dave got nose to nose with Cy. Before he could say anything, Patty put her hand on Dave's shoulder and said, "I got this Dad, I'm not a little girl anymore. Mr. Long, after all these years, you pick my wedding day to ask me and my parents to forgive you for hurting me fifteen years ago? Why today?"

"Patty, as you get older you realize that tomorrow isn't promised to any of us, and you and your parents have been on my conscience."

Patty looked at her brother and then her parents. "You want my parent's forgiveness and mine so you can feel better, is that right?"

Cy took Karen's hand and said, "Patty, Dave, Mary, DJ, I want us to be like we were when we first met on that day Patty and DJ were running in the back yard as kids."

Dave put his hand on Patty's shoulder and said to her, "Baby, Dad has got this from here, go enjoy your wedding day with your husband."

"Cy, Mary and I thought of you and Karen as more than just neighbors, you were like family. Mary misses her relationship with Karen more than I can say, and that bothers me greatly. The thing that will forever hinder that relationship from continuing, is you and the pain you caused my daughter. Over the years you didn't care you had hurt her, Mary, DJ, or me."

The four of them stood there silent. Then Dave said, "Our friendship has been over for fifteen years. It will never be any more than what it is right now. We are not friends, we are not even neighbors, we are just people who live next to each other with a fence. You did all of this Cy, all of this!"

The Crack in the Mirror

Dave and Mary, Cy and Karen. Two families once close, but now their friendship was a distant memory. One family wanted to be forgiven and have things go back to how things used to be. It's too bad this pothole in the road couldn't be filled and smoothed over...but that's the way it goes, sometimes.

Good neighbors were turned into estranged, unforgiving, strangers. Why? Because the crack between these neighbors was just as high as the fence that had separated them.

CHAPTER 8
Lois & Francis

As a little girl, Francis knew she was different from all the other little girls she played with at school and in the neighborhood. When other little girls were playing with dolls and jumping rope, she was thinking of how much she wanted to be near them and how drawn she was to them. Being a child herself, she didn't understand why she was attracted to girls, she just knew that she was. She was raised in a Southern Baptist home by a single parent, her mother Lois. It was her mother who made this revelation about her daughter feeling drawn to girls, and made it more of an ordeal.

Francis's father left soon after she was born. Her mother was the daughter of a Baptist minister and had unwavering ideals on what was right and what was wrong, and she didn't budge. If the Bible said it was wrong, then it was wrong, end of discussion! Francis knew the mindset of her mother and didn't come to her with these feelings of attraction for girls. For one, she didn't really know what to say or how to say it. The second reason was fear.

Francis entered her teens with a constant rage inside her about her sexuality and dreaded the day her mother would find out. Halfway through her senior year, she got a part-time job at a local convenience store working as a cashier. Graduation was coming up and she needed money for her cap and gown, pictures, class ring, the whole nine yards. She didn't want to ask her mother for the money because she was doing the best she could just to keep a roof over their heads and food on the table.

After three months on the job, a new girl was hired to stock the shelves and fill the coolers, and she was gorgeous! Lydia was from Trinidad and moved to the states with her parents when she was 2 years old. She was tall in stature with a melodic movement in her walk, her skin was cinnamon and flawless with a smile to match.

Francis was so captivated by her that she didn't hear the manager.

"Francis, Arlearn! the manager said. "Come here and meet our new employee, Lydia Thomas."

Francis walked toward Lydia and her manager thinking, *She is so beautiful, I must not stare!* Francis extended her hand and said, "Hi, I'm Francis, it's nice to meet you."

Lydia received Francis's hand and said, "It's nice to meet you, too" and flashed that picture-perfect smile that made Francis swoon just a little.

As the time came to close and balance out her register, Lydia asked Francis to help with something. Lydia was on a stepstool placing items on a shelf and wanted Francis to hand them to her so she wouldn't have to keep getting on and off the step stool. Francis finished closing out her register and came over to Lydia.

"What do you need?"

Lydia looked down at Francis from her perch and said, "Please hand me those cans of soup."

"Sure, here you go." As she looked up to hand the cans of soup to Lydia, her top was loose and Francis could see the shape of Lydia's breasts and she dropped the first can.

"Sorry about that Lydia, I'm so clumsy at times." She tried to laugh it off.

"That's alright Honey," Lydia said laughing. "No harm done.

Francis wanted to keep looking up Lydia's top and at the same time she didn't want to keep looking. But she couldn't help herself. Like steel is drawn to a magnet, she was drawn to Lydia and she was powerless to fight it.

After they stocked the shelf, Lydia thanked her for her help.

Francis smiled and said, "You're welcome, Lydia, I was glad to do it."

Francis caught the bus home, all the way thinking about the view under Lydia's top. Part of her felt bad for enjoying that because it felt a little like she was taking advantage of Lydia. Another part felt like she was the one for her, so it couldn't be wrong. When she came through the doors of her house, she still had Lydia on her mind.

"How was work, anything new and exciting?" Lois asked her daughter.

Francis wanted to scream, "I just found my soul-mate and I'm in love with a woman!" But of course, she simply said, "The store hired a new girl to help out."

Lois smiled, "That's nice, get ready for dinner."

As the two of them ate dinner, Lois was going on and on about who knows what. Francis heard nothing. She was lost in thought about Lydia, her brown sugar goddess!

***

Over the passage of weeks, Francis and Lydia grew as friends; although it was more from Francis's perspective. Lydia was a couple of years older than her so she was living on her own.

With her graduation a few days away, Lydia got Arlene a present. "I hope this is what you want because it's what I want as well"

Francis took the pretty little gold box with a red bow and said, "Thank you, Lydia!" She stood there motionless because she didn't understand what Lydia meant by, "Because it's what I want as well."

Breaking the silence, Lydia said, "Well, are you going to open it?"

"Sure." Her hands shook as she undid the red ribbon. Taking the top off and seeing the contents she looked at Lydia. "A key? A key to what?"

Lydia kissed her on the cheek and said, "It's a key to my house. I want you to have it, I want us to be together."

Francis was speechless and struggling to find words. "If I've misread you all these months, then I'm sorry and I apologize. If you feel about me the way I feel about you, then say something."

The emotion of this was overwhelming her and the tears began to run like water. "I've been in love with you from the first day I saw you."

Lydia kissed her tears and said, "I felt a connection as well that first day, but I didn't know if you were into women."

She laughed and kissed Lydia, fulfilling a desire she had carried for months.

"What do you think about your gift? Is this something you want?"

Francis kissed her again and said. "More than anything. But my mother will be crushed!"

"She doesn't know you're gay?" "

No, she doesn't, and I don't know how to tell her!"

"I'll help you if you want me too?"

"Thank you," Francis said as the two of them got lost in each other.

***

After graduation, she had planned to work full time at the store and get her own place. But now plans had changed. She didn't plan on falling in love with Lydia, but she did. She didn't plan on living with another woman, but she was. She didn't plan on "coming out" to her mother, but she had too. Telling her mother— a church going, God-fearing woman—that her daughter was in love with another woman would almost kill her. Painful as this may be, it has to be done. What was the alternative? Deny her sexuality and the woman she loved and be miserable and unhappy? Or, tell the truth and build a life with someone who loved her and made her happy?

As she approached the front steps of her mother's house, she clutched and drew strength from Lydia's house key. She would need all the strength she could muster to break her mother's heart. She drew on the love she felt for Lydia and the love she knew Lydia felt for her to move her feet toward the door.

When she opened the door, Lois greeted her with her standard, "How was work, anything new and exciting?"

She thought, *Boy, is there ever!* She hung her coat and asked her mother to sit down because she needed to talk to her.

"This sounds serious, what is it Francis?"

She took a deep breath, clutched her house key tightly, and told her mother she was gay and in love and moving out after graduation to live with the woman she loved. Lois was a dark-skinned woman born and raised in Huntsville, Alabama, in the Bible belt, so she did not take her news well. As dark as she was, her face appeared to turn white from the shock of Francis's words.

"How could you do such a thing Francis?" yelled Lois as she began to pace back and forth. "You know what the Bible says about homosexuality. It's wrong! Read Leviticus 18:22 girl!"

"Mama, being gay isn't something I chose to be, it's who I am, I was born this way just like you were born the way you are, can't you see that?"

Lois stopped pacing and got eyeball to eyeball with her. "All I know is what my Bible tells me and that's all I need to know!"

Francis was crying so hard she was shaking all over. Lois took two steps and turned back toward her daughter and said, "You don't have to wait until you graduate to move, you can get out now you ungodly piece of filth!"

Those words were more than she could bear. She grabbed her coat and said, "This is the last time you will ever see me. Your religion means more to you than your daughter, so enjoy your God because you've lost your daughter."

***

20 Years Later

Francis and Lydia were still together and in love. On a cool crisp Saturday before Thanksgiving, she and Lydia were shopping for all the fixings for a fine Thanksgiving dinner. Lydia liked pecan pie and she wanted to make one for her.

While she looked over the pie crusts in the freezer section, she heard a familiar voice, "Francis, how are you doing girl? I haven't seen you in years!"

She turned and recognized the owner of the voice. "How are you Mrs. Fletcher? It has been a long time."

Mrs. Fletcher had lived next door to Francis and her mother.

"I see by your cart, you're getting ready for Thanksgiving!"

"Yes ma'am, I sure am," she said as she looked around for Lydia.

"You know, your mother misses you something terrible, don't you?"

"Mrs. Fletcher, that wasn't my choice to cut her out of my life, she made that decision, not me!" Just then Lydia showed up with a turkey and sweet potatoes and she could tell the conversation was getting heavy. She introduced Lydia to Mrs. Fletcher as her life partner and the person she loved.

"So, you're the one?"

Before Lydia could respond, Francis said, "The one what? What do you mean by that?" Lydia knew how sensitive and protective she could get if questioned about her relationship with her, so she took her hand and the cart and moved on.

"That old bitch, who I'm with ain't none of her business!"

Lydia kissed her and told her, "Don't let other people steal your joy Honey, don't give them that power, o.k.?"

"You're right Lydia, it only matters what people say if I allow it to matter. You are so wise, that's one of the reasons why I love you so much."

***

Thanksgiving came and went, a New Year came and went as well. And with the coming of that new year was some bad news, Lois had cancer.

She was never big on going to the doctor because she believed her God would heal and protect her from sickness. When she got to the point that the pain was just too much and she finally did see a doctor, the cancer was out of control. Mrs. Fletcher was somewhat of a busy-body, tending to everybody's business but her own, but she meant well. She knew Francis had no idea what was going on with her mother and she felt she should know, regardless of what was going on between them.

Mrs. Fletcher had a daughter who had graduated with Francis and she asked her if she could find out where she lived. Her daughter said she would try. A couple of weeks went by and Mrs. Fletcher got the information she wanted so she went to the address she was given. She knocked on the door and Lydia opened it.

"You're the woman from the store, what do you want? I'm not going to let you upset Francis!"

"Dear, I'm not here to upset her or you, but there is something she should know"

"What is it? I can tell her!"

"It's about her mother, is she here?"

Lydia softened her tone. "Yes, she's here, come in and I'll get her."

Mrs. Fletcher followed Lydia into the living room where Francis looked shocked to see her old neighbor.

"Mrs. Fletcher, what's this all about, something about my mother?"

"Yes Dear, your mother is not well, she has cancer and it's too advanced for treatment."

"So, what are you telling me, that she's dying?" Francis reached for Lydia.

"Yes Francis, that's what I'm saying. I know you didn't know and I felt you should."

"I'll be on my way now," Mrs. Fletcher said as she headed back to the door. "Don't wait too long to go and see her, she doesn't have much time."

Francis hugged her and promised to see her mother soon. Lydia held her tight.

"What do you want to do?"

"Right now, I need to think by myself for a minute," she said.

"Ok, I'm going the store for some things, you need anything?"

"Just you!" as she hugged and kissed her goodbye.

After all these years of being disowned by her, how am I supposed to feel? She asked herself. Her mother had turned her back on her and denounced her lifestyle and the person she loved, so how was she supposed to feel about her mother dying? Part of her hated her mother and another part loved her because she was still her mother.

When Lydia came back from the store, she told her she had decided to go and see the mother she had once vowed never to see again.

"I think that's the right thing to do, Honey. And I know it's not an easy thing for you."

Francis signed, "No it's not, but I feel I have too, you know?"

"I understand Honey, let's watch a movie, I'll pop some popcorn ok?" Francis smiled and said, "That sounds good."

Two days later, she and Lydia went to see Lois. Francis loved Lydia and she didn't care who didn't like it, including her mother. Lydia was a part of her life and she was not going to hide her so others could feel comfortable. As she walked up to the door, she was nervous, scared, and a bunch of other emotions as well, but she was determined to do this with the woman she loved.

She ranged the bell and Lois came to the door, peaked through the curtains. Francis heard her say, "Oh my Lord in heaven," as Lois opened the door. They both started crying and hugging; forgetting Lydia was even standing there. After what seemed like hours, Lois looked at Lydia and asked, "What is she doing here Francis?"

Mother, this is Lydia, the woman I love and I am not ashamed of her or our love and I will not act like I am."

"She is not welcomed in my house! And if you want her, you are not welcomed in my house either!"

"Well, I guess we'll be going. Take care mother. This will definitely be the last time that you see me, EVER!"

Having been quiet all this time, Lydia had enough of Lois hurting the person she loved. She could no longer hold her tongue.

"You have missed out on so much happiness with your daughter, but because of your ways, you have denied yourself, and her, a relationship both of you would have benefited from," Lydia said. "I love her even if you don't, and I'll hold her even if you won't. Goodbye, Lois."

The Crack in the Mirror

Soon after that, Lois died. Francis couldn't bring herself to go to the funeral. She reasoned, "if my mother didn't want me, or the person I love around her in life, why should I and her, be around my mother in death?"

To some people that may sound cold. But Francis wanted to try to mend things with her mother in the end. Her mother was set in her ways about Francis's sexual orientation. That crack in their relationship was more than Lois could accept, and something Francis felt she had no choice in.

CHAPTER 9
Louis & Trey

When one becomes a father, there is no "How-To" manual. There is no instructional video. A man can only try to do the best he can with what he has and hope for the best. Parents may disappoint their child at times, and they, in turn, may disappoint their parents; but both forge ahead. Trey was born Louis Franklin Simmons III. He earned his nicknamed from his grandfather and father. Like his father and his grandfather before him, he was expected to follow in his namesake's footsteps and become a cop. There was just one problem, he didn't want too.

There was nothing wrong with being a police officer, but Trey's interests were elsewhere. When he was 4 years old, his mother sat him on the piano stool with her while she played. As he got older, she taught him to play. She was an accomplished musician on the piano, violin, and flute.

Trey was a natural. He inherited his mother's talent and love of music and wanted to pursue a career in music after studying at Juilliard in New York. That was his dream; a dream he shared only with his mother. His father would denounce his dream because he felt music as not a "manly" profession in his eyes. Louis had definite ideas of what was considered "manly" and what was not. Being a cop was the ultimate in his eyes. Being a musician, well, that was fine for women. Louis said men needed to get "real jobs," not pluck on some strings or pound on piano keys like children.

One day, before Trey came home, Louis took the mail from the box. He noticed the envelope was addressed to Trey. It was from The Juilliard School of Performing Arts in New York City. Louis was enraged, the plan for Trey's life after high school meant nothing to him. The family tradition, meant nothing to him.

"How could he do this to me?" Louis quickly folded up the letter and put it in his pocket. He went outside and sat on the bench he built with his father some years ago. When Trey came home, he asked Louis about the mail.

Making an effort to not show his anger, Louis said, "Yeah, it's on the table in the kitchen."

"Ok, Dad," Trey said as he went into the house. Trey came back outside to his father. "That's all the mail?"

Louis let his temper out somewhat and barked, "What you see there is what is there, you expecting something?"

Trey didn't know what to make of his father's outburst, so he just said, "No, I was just wondering, that's all." The truth was, Trey was expecting time-sensitive news from Julliard. If he was accepted he needed to make arrangements regarding financial aid and other monetary obligations he would have to fulfill.

Trey's mother was aware he had applied to Julliard despite the objections of her husband. She knew of her son's deep love of music and that nothing would bring him more joy than following his dream.

***

Juilliard sent a second letter with "Final Attempt" stamped in red. Places like Juilliard were not going to beg students as they had so many other people who wanted to get in. Again, Louis got the mail first and this time he opened the letter and read it much to his displeasure. Juilliard was stating that Trey had been accepted, but they needed to hear from him a week ago. This was the final letter.

The letter read: "If there is no written correspondence, phone call or email received by admissions within a week upon receiving this final letter, we will assume you are no longer interested in attending Juilliard." Louis smiled and thought, *All I got to do is make sure he never finds out Juilliard sent these letters and he won't have a choice but to be a cop.*

***

Two months had gone by and Trey was disappointed and hurt.

"Mama, why hasn't Juilliard contacted me? It's been almost three months since I applied, what's wrong?"

Trey's mother hugged him and said, "Trey, don't wait any longer to hear from them, let Juilliard hear from you."

"I'm going to do just that, I'm calling right now! Thanks Mama, you always know just what to do."

Trey called Juilliard and asked for admissions. He was transferred to an admissions officer, Mrs. Rollins.

"Good morning Mrs. Rollins, my name is Louis Franklin Simmons III and I'm wondering why I haven't heard anything from you regarding my being accepted or not, at Juilliard?"

"Can you please hold while I access your application for admittance?"

"Yes," said Trey, knowing this could take a while. Surprisingly the wait was not long. Trey learned that his application was in the terminate file due to non-compliance.

Mrs. Rollins came back on line. "Mr. Simmons, I'm sorry, but due to no response to the two letters we sent you, we had to no longer consider you for admission to Juilliard, I'm sorry."

"What letters are you talking about?" screamed Trey on the verge of tears.

"The two letters we sent to your house. The first one informed you of your acceptance. The second letter reiterating what the first letter said plus letting you know that further non-compliance of more than a week would void your acceptance."

"Are you sure you sent the letters to the right address, because I never saw them?" said Trey feeling sick to his stomach.

"They were sent to the address on your application Mr. Simmons." She read the address and it was in fact, correct. There was nothing to be done about it now. "Again Mr. Simmons, I'm truly sorry."

Trey could barely talk, but managed to say, "Thank you, Mrs. Rollins," and hung up the phone.

As he sat there in disbelief, he kept thinking, *What could have happened? Did the letters get lost as mail sometimes does? Maybe they got delivered to a house address similar?*

What ever happened, it didn't matter now because it's too late, his dream is over before it had a chance to begin.

"Well, what did you find out?" his mother asked.

"I'm not going to Juilliard."

"Why?" she asked as she held his hands in hers. "They didn't accept you?"

"No, that's not it, I was accepted." Trey released her grip and looked out the window.

"Then what's the problem?"

"They said I didn't respond back to them in a timely manner and therefore, lost my chance to go to Juilliard."

Looking puzzled, his mother said, "How can you respond back to someone when you haven't received anything to respond too?"

"Juilliard sent two letters letting me know I had been accepted and that I needed to respond in a timely manner. When I didn't, they assumed I wasn't interested."

"Of course, you're interested! It's been your dream to go to Juilliard ever since you knew there was a Juilliard."

"Mama, I can only think of one other possibility for what has happened, Dad."

"What do you mean?"

Trey sat his mother down on the sofa. "Since I was old enough to walk and talk, what have I been told by Dad that I was going to be?"

His mother said in a low voice, "A cop."

"Yeah, just like him and just like grandfather, that's all I've ever heard."

"So, what are you getting at Trey?"

"I think Dad got a hold of those letters and kept them from me so I wouldn't go to Juilliard and that I would be a cop like he wanted all along, that's what I think!"

"Trey no! Your father loves you, he would never do something intentionally to hurt you?"

"I don't think he cares about what I want, it's all about what he wants. And besides, he doesn't respect music as a career for a man anyway."

"I hope you're wrong about this son," his mother said as she hugged and kissed him.

"I hope I'm wrong too Mama, but I don't think I am."

Louis pulled up in the driveway and Trey and his mother looked at each other like people do, when something heavy is about to go down.

"What's up Dad, how was your day?" asked Trey.

Louis looked at him with raised eyebrows because Trey never asked him how was his day as a cop. "It was alright, just dealing with the local human scum, that's all."

It was these types of responses by Louis that made Trey not ask what kind of day his father had. "Why are you asking me about my day, you never ask me that?" said Louis sitting down in his favorite chair.

Trey walked closer to his father. "When a man is doing something he loves for a living, his day should be very fulfilling, don't you think Dad?"

"I suppose so," Louis said, wondering what this conversation was all about. "Is there something on your mind Trey you want to talk about?"

Trey's mother didn't like the vibes in the room she was getting from Louis or Trey so she tried to be a buffer. "Shania had her baby yesterday, a boy, he looks just like Randy!"

Shania was her niece, but changing the subject didn't last.

"Well son, you got something to say to me? Spit it out!"

Both Trey and Louis were on their feet, looking each other in the eye; neither of them blinked.

"I don't have anything to say to you, but I do have something to ask of you."

"So, ask away," said Louis with his arms folded.

"Did you see some letters from Juilliard addressed to me?"

Louis knew his next response was not going to be received well and he didn't care. "Yeah, I saw the letters and I threw them away because you are going to the police academy, end of stor.y!"

Trey turned to his mother and said, "You hear that Mama, he isn't even going to lie and say he didn't see them."

"How could you do this to your son? This was his dream, his life, you bastard!"

"Careful woman, you watch how you talk to me!" said Louis with balled-up fists. "I did it for your own good Trey, you were born to be a cop just like me and your grandfather."

Trey never cussed at his father in his life, but self control was now out the window. "How the fuck is what you did for my own good Dad?" I don't want to be a cop, I never have, that's your dream, not mine! You and grandfather planned out my entire life without once considering that maybe I had other plans for my life. You have destroyed my dream and disrespected my wants and desires. I'm getting out of your house. Run somebody else's life because you're not going to run mine! I love you Mama, but I got to go!'"

The Crack in the Mirror

Trey left his parents house. He couldn't forgive his father for destroying his dream. His father couldn't ask for forgiveness because he was too prideful.

Both remained that way until Louis died.

The crack between them was too much to overcome.

CHAPTER 10
Roma & Shelby

Sisters can be really close. Such was the case of Roma and her younger sister Vicky who were tight as a pair of pantyhose two sizes too small. Vicky thought of Roma like she was her second mother instead of her older sister, because she was so protective and always looked out for her.

Roma and her husband Justin, had no children because Roma couldn't. She always felt she was depriving Justin of that gift. Vicky and her husband Roy, had one daughter Shelby, who was the joy of their lives. Vicky and Roy had always wanted to travel out west and see "God's Country" as they were fond of saying; the Grand Canyon, the Rocky Mountains and the raging white-water of the Colorado River. Living in Muncie, Indiana, these sights seemed a million miles away, but they were determined to see them one day.

That day finally came when Shelby was 10 years old. As the family headed west to fulfill their long-awaited dream, suddenly disaster struck. Just outside St. Louis on I-270 West on the by-pass going around the city, a semi-truck changed lanes abruptly and forced Roy to jump into the next lane. He hit the bumper of a car that caused him to lose control and hit the concrete divider. He and Vicky were killed. Shelby suffered a broken arm and bruises, but survived.

Roma was devastated by the news that her baby sister was gone. How could she get through this! What would become of Shelby? Roma didn't need to think twice about what was going to happen with Shelby, she would live with her and Justin, case closed. Shelby wanted that also. She loved her "Aunt Ro,"and was thrilled to be with her and her Uncle Justin. Shelby made the adjustments that kids make when they move to a new place, go to a new school and she made new friends. But Athens, Georgia wasn't Muncie. People were more laid back, easy going and friendly. She reasoned it must be a Southern thing.

***

10 Years Later

Shelby was turning into quite an attractive young lady. She had her mother's hazel eyes and wavey, black hair; and the boys noticed too. Now 17 years old, she was in her junior year of high school. While boys were taking notice, so was

Uncle Justin. Shelby began to notice her Uncle looking at her in a way that didn't feel right to her. She thought, *maybe I'm reading too much into this.*

She was in her room one evening studying with her door open when her Uncle passed by in the hall. The shadow from the desk lamp projected her silouette on the wall. Her Uncle backed up and stood in the hallway taking in the sight of his now obsession. When Shelby was finally aware he was standing in the hall at her doorway she was startled.

"Oh! Hey Uncle J, I didn't see you there!"

"I was just passing by Shell." He lied, he had been standing there for five minutes or more, but Shelby hadn't noticed.

"What are you reading?" he asked as he walked into her room, uninvited.

"I have a chemistry test tomorrow and I need to read some chapters."

Justin got closer to her and put his hand on her left shoulder. He began to kneed it like dough. Shelby didn't like his touch and dipped her shoulder so his hand slid off.

"I'm sure you will do fine on your test, Honey, you're smart just like your Aunt Ro." With that, Justin walked out of her room. "Goodnight Shell."

"Goodnight Uncle J," Shelby replied. *That felt weird* Shelby thought. W*as Uncle J being more than just a concerned Uncle?*"

Some days later, Shelby got a new sofa for her room as the old one had broken down and was really uncomfortable. She had a rather large room as her Aunt Ro wanted her to be as relaxed and comfortable as possible. It was her room and what ever she wanted to do with it was up to her; it was her space. As she pushed the old sofa out of her room to make room for the new one, it got stuck in the doorway.

"It came in here without difficulty, so what's the problem?" She said to herself. She pushed and crawled underneath it to get in front of it to pull it but it wouldn't budge.

Hearing all the noise, her uncle came upstairs. "Shell, what's with all the noise?"

Shelby wiped some sweat from her forehead. "I'm trying to move this old sofa out of my room to make room for a new one I bought. Shelby was left a nice sum of money from her parent's death.

"Okay, let me help you." Justin pulled from the other side as she pushed. The sofa woldn't budge.

After five minutes of pushing and pulling, Shelby said, "Uncle J it's not moving, now what?"

"I got an idea. Let me get on that side with you."

After barely squeezing underneath to get to where Shelby was, Justin said, "That was a tight fit, as some things can be."

Shelby looked at him puzzled and said, "Yeah, I guess so."

"So, what's your idea Uncle J?"

Looking at her and talking about the sofa, Justin was getting closer and closer to Shelby and she was starting to get uneasy. "I was thinking that if we take the back off we can get it through the doorway with no problem, what do you think?"

Shelby was ready for him to be gone from her personal space so she said, "Sure, whatever it takes to get it out."

"I'm going to need you to do something Shell. Steady the base while I push the back off, can you do that?"

"Yeah, I can do that." She got down on the floor on her knees to steady the base.

"Are you ready?"

"Yeah, I'm ready, this is getting heavy!"

Justin had moved the sofa slightly so it wouldn't fall, but with the weight on Shelby, she couldn't let go of it at the base either. Suddenly, Shelby felt her Uncle's hands under her shirt cupping her breasts.

"Uncle J! What are you doing!" she screamed.

Fully consumed by lust, Justin said, "Something I've been wanting to do for a long time." His hands moved from her breasts to between her legs as she began to sob uncontrollably.

"Stop! Uncle J please stop!"

There would be no stopping. Justin was blind from his lust and he heard nothing and saw nothing, only the object of his twisted desire. "I know you've noticed me looking at you ever since you were 15, haven't you?" He pulled her pants down and ripped her panties off.

"Uncle J, please don't do this! PLEASE!"

Her words fell on deaf ears as Justin raped Shelby, his wife's sister's daughter, his niece.

When he was through satisfying his lust, he told Shelby, "Don't think about telling your Aunt Ro about what happened! She won't believe you anyway."

Zipping up his pants he said with a grin on his face, "You know how much she loves me, do you think she will take your word over mine?"

Moving her out of the way of the sofa, he pushed it on through the doorway and into the hall. "There you go, sofa moved! Oh, you better get cleaned up before your aunt gets home. I'll take care of the sofa."

Shelby was crushed. How could her uncle violate her so brutally and act like nothing had happened? Justin got rid of the old sofa just before the new one arrived. But she couldn't care less about it. She showered, washed her body over and over trying to get her Uncle off of her and from inside of her.

What if I'm pregnant? What would that do to Aunt Ro, in light of the fact that she couldn't have children!

Ro was out of town for her job, but she would be home later that evening.

Upon her arrival, she sensed tension in the air. "Anything new or exciting happen while I was gone?" Ro asked while passing the mashed potatoes during dinner.

Shelby in a low voice said, "You know that sofa you and I were looking at that I wanted for my room?"

"Yes dear, I remember it."

"Well, I bought it and it was delivered this afternoon."

Ro touched Shelby's hand and said, "That's wonderful Dear, how did you get the old one out?"

Shelby paused and Justin spoke up, "I helped her get it out of her room and took it to the dump."

Ro looked at Justin. "That was so sweet of you Justin, wasn't it Shell?"

Fighting back tears, Shelby said, "Yes Aunt Ro, it was sweet."

Feeling like he had to say something, Justin said, "It was nothing, just helping out my niece, that's all."

Shelby was livid by Justin's nonchalant response, *It was nothing! It was nothing! You raped me you lying motherfucker and you say it was nothing!"* Shelby grabbed her glass and drank some water.

Shelby kept thinking about what her Uncle said: "Don't think about telling your Aunt Ro about what happened, she won't believe you anyway."

Was he right? She wondered, *would Aunt Ro believe a lying rapist over me, even if it were her husband?*

***

Shelby's mood changed during the coming months and she began seriously thinking about moving to get away from her Uncle.

Shelby was downstairs in the basement doing laundry one day when Justin came down the stairs. "What do you want Uncle J?" she asked as she backed up slightly.

"I don't want anything Baby, I just wanted to say Hi. "We don't talk much anymore and I miss that."

Shelby had started carrying a knife on her after Justin raped her months before, she was determined there would not be a second time. "You know something Uncle J, when you rape someone, they kind of don't want to be around you, you know?"

Justin laughed a little and said, "Come on Shell, that was just a little misunderstanding, that's all."

Shelby had the knife under some towels as she slid her hand under them to grip it and said, "A little misunderstanding? Man, are you for real? You raped me you son-of-a-bitch, that's not a misunderstanding!"

Shelby could feel her fear turn to anger as she began to tell her Uncle about himself. "You tricked me in letting you supposedly help me, you forcefully grabbed my breasts, was that a misunderstanding? You put your hands between my legs and gripped and groped my pussy, was that a misunderstanding Uncle J?"

She was saying everything she wanted to say since the rape and she let it all out. "When you forced your dick inside me Uncle J, was that a misunderstanding too?" Shelby felt her grip get tighter around the knife handle, and like her mother, her face got really red and warm when she was angry. "I can't hear you Uncle J, was all of that a big misunderstanding!"

Justin had never seen this side of Shelby before and it made him a little nervous and excited at the same time. "Hey, Shell, we can get through this, right? There's no need to be shouting rape."

Shelby looked him in the eye and said, "When you force someone to have sex, it's rape, plain and simple asshole!"

"You better watch how you talk to me, I'm your Uncle, you are under my roof."

Shelby laughed. "You are not my Uncle, you are my Aunt's sorry-ass husband, that's all you are!"

Justin was mad now after all the things Shelby said.

"I'll teach you to disrespect me in my own house you little bitch!" Justin noticed all the time Shelby was talking that her right hand stayed in one spot, under the towels, so he figured she had something under them. He grabbed her right hand from under the towels and cut his self on the knife screaming at her, "Look at what you did to me!" He ripped her blouse and pulled at her bra and broke the straps.

Shelby thought, *This can't be happening again, I won't let it!*

Just then Ro came down the basement stairs. "I thought you had to go in to the office Honey?" said Justin, out of breath.

"What the hell is going on down here Justin,? Shelby?"

"Baby, Shelby has been coming on to me for months now and I didn't want to tell you because I didn't want to hurt you."

Shelby burst into tears and said, "Aunt Ro he's lying, he tried to rape me again!"

Ro turned and walked over to Shelby and said, "What do you mean, again?"

Shelby wiped her face and said, "Remember when you had to go out of town for your job a few months ago?"

"Yes."

"Uncle J raped me Aunt Ro and he told me that if I told you, you wouldn't believe me, but I'm telling you the truth, he raped me!"

Ro stood there motionless, starring blankly at the washer and dryer. She finally found the courage to ask, "Is it true Justin, did you rape Shelby that time I was out of town?"

"No baby, how could you think I could do such a thing? You know I love you?"

Ro looked at Shelby and asked Justin, "Why is she half naked with blood on her?"

"She came on to me like she's been doing and I pushed her away from me and I tore her clothes. She then pulled a knife on me because I rejected her!"

Shelby ran to Ro and cried, "Aunt Ro he is lying to you, I would never do anything like that to hurt you, you have been like a mother to me, I love you!"

Ro looked at Justin then back at Shelby. Ro faced Shelby and said, "You're 18 now and old enough to be on your own. You still have enough money left from your parent's life insurance to get you started on your own. I want you out, NOW!"

"But Aunt Ro!"

"Don't Aunt Ro me, Slut! Get out of my house!"

Shelby ran up the stairs crying and screaming, "I'm telling the truth, he's lying, he's lying!" She gathered the things that she could carry and went to a friend's house.

***

Shelby later moved back to Muncie, Indiana and rekindled old relationships she had made when she was a child. One boy who she grew up with and knew since she was in the third grade, heard she was back in town. They started dating and were married a year later, and started a family.

Roma discovered, some years after Shelby had left, that her niece was telling the truth. She wanted to make things right between her and Shelby, but was it too late?

Roma heard Shelby had moved back to Muncie and got her phone number and called her. When Shelby answered, the voice on the other end sounded familiar.

Shelby was in disbelief. "Is this who I think it is?"

"Yes, Shelby it's your Aunt Ro, I need to talk to you if I can?" Roma didn't know how her call would be received, but she felt she had to apologize to Shelby and beg for her forgiveness. "Shelby, honey, I know I hurt you by not believing you when you needed me too. But he was my husband, you can understand that can't you?"

Shelby took a deep breath. "Roma, here is what I understand. I understand your husband raped me when I was a 17-year-old kid. I understand he tried to do it again and you saw with your own eyes my torn clothes and you still refused to believe me. That's what I understand Roma!"

Shelby felt a tear sliding down her cheek as she said, "You stopped being Aunt Ro the day you stopped believing in me."

There was silence on both ends of the phone. Finally Roma said, "I want us to be *us* again, what do you think Shelby? Uncle Justin passed away two years ago and I've been thinking about you a lot."

Shelby gathered her composure and calmly said, "Roma, I'm happy, I'm married to a wonderful man, unlike that piece of shit you had. I have a beautiful son and daughter, so no; we can't be *us* again!

"Can't you forgive me Shelby? I'm sorry sweetheart!"

"Forgiveness is not in my heart Roma, goodbye."

The Crack in the Mirror

Shelby was hurt deeply by her aunt's denial of the sexual assault committed by Justin.

Roma wanted to correct their relationship, but the crack was too wide for Shelby.

CONCLUSION

After reading this book about the different relationships depicted, did you see one or some that you could relate too? If you did, you are not alone and if you didn't, you soon will.

The purpose of this book was to point out the human element in relationships that we as humans bring into them, for better or for worse. Hurting those closest to us is a very human thing. Not seeing the hurt coming from those closest to us is a common thing. The reason it is a common thing not to see the hurt coming from a loved one is because your guard is down.

You are not expecting a deliberate painful blow to be delivered, like the one with Trey and his father, Louis, who hurt his son by destroying letters that could have changed Trey's life. Or, how Earl was totally blindsided by his sister Linda's greed. The closer someone is to you, the easier it may be for them to hurt you... and the greater and the longer the pain will last.

Relationships are complex and run hot and cold as they continue throughout the span of our lives. It's this ebb and flow of human emotions, meant to support or tear down the object of focus, that makes all of us show our true colors. Over the years, Linda acted like she loved her brother, but when money entered into the picture, "HER" true colors shone through!

If you saw yourself—on either end of any of these relationships—can you change before it's too late? If you are the one who caused the crack, can you admit it and strive to do what is necessary to make it right? If you are the one who was hurt, can you find forgiveness for the one who hurt you?

As you have seen from the relationships in the book, both parties let things lie as they ended and did nothing to make amends. It wasn't that they *wouldn't* they just *couldn't,* because the crack was too wide and too deep.

These stories didn't have happy endings because life doesn't always give us happy endings. Even though the relationships were damaged, the people were strong enough to move past the emotional wreckage and get on with their lives. We all have hurt and have been hurt by loved ones. Can we get over the crack in our own mirror? If you can, you are most fortunate. If you can't, life goes on and you have to go on with it.

ABOUT THE AUTHOR

James J. Smith is known for his controversial commentary on everything from race relations to politics. In addition to being an author, he is a newspaper columnist, radio cohost, and public speaker.

His previous works include: *Stirrings From My Soul, Reflections, As I See it: Poetry to Enlighten the Mind, Encourage the Spirit, Lift the Heart, Sunk By the Navy: My Personal Experience as a Black Sailor in the Navy During the Vietnam Era,* and *There's a Thin Line Between a Pimp and a Preacher.*

James resides in Battle Creek, Michigan with his wife Camille.

54200921R00046

Made in the USA
Columbia, SC
29 March 2019